The Citadel: A Ransom & Fortune Adventure

Volume 3

Michelle Miles

This is a work of fiction. All characters, organizations and events portrayed in this novel are either products of the author's imagination or used fictitiously.

THE CITADEL: A RANSOM & FORTUNE ADVENTURE

Cover Design by Erin Dameron-Hill

ISBN: 978-1-7343068-0-4

The Citadel

A Ransom & Fortune Adventure, Volume 3
This title was previously published as part one of
A Break in Time.

As Skye Ransom and Dane Fortune time jump for the third time, they leave the frozen tundra of wintertime behind, hoping to land in their own century. That hope is crushed when they wake up in a jungle with oppressive humidity and a native tribe who mistakes Skye for the Goddess of Fire. Arriving at the tribe's village, they're introduced to Dr. Charles Ridgewood who gives them the impression he is not what he appears.

While waiting for the time bender to reset, they're honored guests of the Citadel's royal family. But when Dane falls ill, and Skye is captured, the true identity of Dr. Ridgewood is revealed and an old enemy returns to finish a job he started.

Now separated, the two have to reunite before they're lost to each other forever.

Prologue

Ark Crane arrived in a cold dismal future populated with strange people who acted as though they had never seen technology. And perhaps they hadn't. They carried crude and rudimentary weapons. He hated the frozen tundra almost as much as he hated his job. But his job allowed him to continue to live. He'd do just about anything for that.

He tracked his prey for two days while freezing his ass off. His fingers, his toes, his face were all numb from the cold. He cursed this frozen wasteland and wondered if it was better to off himself than to continue…until he heard the rumors of a flame-haired beauty traveling with a healer.

He almost snorted. A healer? Dane Fortune was as far from healer as he was.

Ark followed a primitive nomadic tribe heading north towards what they called civilization. It was clear to him he couldn't blend in with them. Not with his modern snow gear and weapons. At night, he kept to the darkness, hovering on the perimeter of their encampment. Watching. Waiting. Listening. When they slept, he stole food and ale, so he wouldn't have to survive on his own.

Finally, he got a break. There was a prophecy about a female human sacrifice on top of a mountain that foretold the uniting of the tribes. The tribe he followed headed there. Ark hoped sticking with them would eventually lead him to Skye and Dane.

The tribe was abuzz about arriving at what they simply called The Bunker the following morning. As they camped for the night, Ark prepared his weapons, stole a whole roasted rabbit, and planned Skye and Dane's murder.

At dawn, he crept away from the camp and made his way to the bunker. As he crested the ridge, he saw them. The flame-haired beauty and her healer.

Ark was one lucky bastard.

He smirked and aimed the handgun. Maybe a warning shot was all they needed, but he didn't want to give them time to bolt. He fired.

Dane shoved the girl to the snow with a grunt. She shrieked his name.

This was too easy. Ark changed to the AR-15, keeping them pinned to the ground in a shower of bullets while he advanced. The girl dove for a shiny object. Ark picked up speed. He couldn't let them time jump and released another round. A second later, there was a flash and they were gone.

He swore as he jogged to the place they vacated. A few drops of blood stained the snow. Ark grinned.

"Gotcha."

At least he hit one of them. Likely Dane when he shoved the girl to the ground. Ark pulled out his own time bender and dialed in his present day. A push of the button, the flash of the world around him, and he was right back at Janus Force headquarters.

Conner Dade waited on the other side in the time jump room seated at the computer that tracked him through time. Charles Ridgewood stood behind him with a grim expression on his face.

"You failed," Ridgewood announced as soon as he arrived. His British tone was clipped with a hint of annoyance.

Ark peeled out of the cold weather gear, leaving it in a wet heap on the floor. "This time."

Ridgewood's wrinkled face was less than friendly. "This time? And do you think there will be a next time?"

"If you want your faulty time machine back, yeah, I do."

"They time jumped," Conner said. "I found their new location." His face paled.

"And where might that be?" Impatience laced Ridgewood's clipped tone.

"This is even hard for me to believe, but…" Conner swallowed hard as he looked up at the two of them. "But something went haywire with their device. I can't pinpoint the exact date."

Ridgewood huffed out a breath and folded his arms across his chest. "What does that mean?"

"It means they managed to break through the time barrier in a way I've never seen, nor can truly explain. It's like time bent around them and they crossed into a…parallel universe. They crossed into a new reality."

Ark's brows knit together as he glanced between the two of them. The older man's blue eyes narrowed as he glared at Conner.

"Explain."

"If you believe what some physicists believe, space-time is flat and goes on forever. There are an infinite number of universes. Perhaps even some parallel universes," Conner said. "But it looks as though they managed to jump through one of those. As if time folded in on itself and bent around them, forcing them to this alternate world."

Ridgewood's stare on Conner was cold. "Where are they, Conner?"

He took a deep breath. "Honestly, sir, I have no idea, but my best guess is they made it to a parallel universe of the Mayan Empire somewhere in Ancient Belize."

~ ⌚ ~

In Rural Pennsylvania

Thomas Hardy parked the old Chevy pick-up and then headed into the small grocery store. He tried to avoid going into town but since he only had one egg and a can of tuna left, he had to buy food or starve. He preferred not starving.

As far as the NSA and DARPA were concerned, Thomas Hardy was officially off the grid. During his self-imposed exile from the real world, he created enough fake IDs and passports that should he need a fast exit from the U.S., he could do it. And since he knew his savings was about to be completely drained, he started doing odd jobs to maintain cashflow.

And still eat. Eating was important.

But not nearly as important as bandwidth. Using his wits, computer smarts and fake ID, he set up his lab in the abandoned barn of an old farm in Amish country to keep an eye on Skye and Dane's time traveling. So far, he hadn't been able to help them get back home. He'd barely been able to track them. He has no idea how he was going to get them home.

Their last time travel landed them in a strange place he couldn't explain. One minute, they were in futuristic Russia, the next they were in a time and place he had never seen before. It was a puzzle. One in which he couldn't fit the pieces. One he had to figure out, sooner rather than later, if he intended to get them home.

Shopping for food—he hoped—would help him work it out. Thinking about what brand of tuna to buy would get his subconscious working.

All this ran through his mind as he wheeled his cart through the aisles buying only what he could afford. He noticed the young man in the red baseball cap on the cookie and snacks aisle, but didn't think anything of it. Until he noticed the same young man at paper goods eyeing him. He didn't have a cart and didn't appear to be shopping.

Warning bells went off in his head as Thomas stood at the plastic wrap wondering what he was supposed to do next. He grabbed a box and tossed it into the cart even though he didn't have a need for it. He strolled down the rest of the aisle heading for the meat department. Red baseball cap boy followed.

What should he do? Abandon his cart and get the hell out of there? Finish shopping and pretend he didn't see him? He couldn't allow the guy to follow him back to the farmhouse. No one knew where he was. He wanted to keep it that way.

Staying calm, Thomas tossed meat into his cart and then headed to frozen foods. Still, he followed.

At the freezer, with shaking hands, Thomas grabbed a handful of frozen dinners and chunked them in the cart. Red baseball cap approached him, pretending to ponder purchasing frozen lasagna. Thomas knew he had to act.

He spun his cart around and slammed it into the guy, ramming him against the glass door of the freezer. Red baseball cap sucked in a sharp breath as Thomas shoved the cart into him, keeping him pinned.

"Who are you and what do you want?"

"I-I…"

Crap. It was a kid. He couldn't be more than twenty. His baby face was smooth and devoid facial hair. Fear rimmed his wide eyes.

"Y-your Thomas Hardy."

"Shut your mouth." Thomas leaned forward and whisper-shouted the words.

"My name is Harold. I want to help you."

He narrowed his eyes. "Help me do what?"

The boy glanced around to see if anyone was listening. Thomas was aware of customers giving him sidelong curious glances, but refusing to get involved.

"I can't tell you here. You better let me go before they call the manager." He jerked his head in the direction of one of the customers.

Thomas saw the older woman scurry down the aisle and disappear. He pulled his cart back and released the boy. Without another word, he wheeled it down the aisle and headed for the checkout, Harold on his heels. On the way past an endcap of beer, Thomas snagged a six pack. At least he didn't say anything else as they got in line.

The manager appeared next with a fake smile plastered on his face. "Everything all right here?"

Thomas pressed his lips together and gave Harold a glance full of daggers. "My younger brother and I were discussing which frozen dinners to buy. That's all."

The manager looked them both over before giving a faint nod and strolling away. Harold pushed his way to the front of the cart as they were next in line and started unloading the food.

"I don't need your help," Thomas's voice was tight, on edge.

"You need my help more than you realize." He tossed a package of sliced cheese on the conveyor belt as the checker started scanning.

Thomas kept his mouth shut and then elbowed his way past Harold who reached for his wallet.

"I'm paying," the boy said.

"No, you're not."

"I am." When the checker finished, he handed the woman cash. "Say thank you."

Thomas glared and snatched the receipt from the woman. He shoved the cart with full grocery bags and headed for the door. Harold followed him outside to the parking lot.

"You know what? It's okay. You don't have to say thanks. But I'm still going to help you."

To his horror, the boy loaded the bags into the back of the old pick-up.

"Stop it." Thomas charged around the cart and shoved him against the truck, his arm on his chest. "I don't know who you are or what you want, but I don't *need* your help. Or your charity."

"You *do* need my help if you're going to get Skye and Dane home."

Thomas stopped breathing as he stared at the kid, his heart ramming against his chest. Terror danced up his spine. "How do you know about them?"

"I know," was all he said.

Slowly, Thomas removed his arm and stepped back. He raked a hand through his hair and blew out a heavy breath. "Get in the damn truck."

It was against his better judgement, but he drove Harold down the street to the local diner. He didn't know this kid. He couldn't trust him. There was no way he was driving him to his hideaway farmhouse until he got more information.

Thomas ordered a coffee. Harold ordered a milkshake and a cheeseburger, cementing his kid-like appearance with a kid-like meal.

"Start talking," Thomas said as soon as the waitress walked away.

"You don't recognize me, do you?" the kid asked.

"If I did, I wouldn't have run you over with my shopping cart."

"Good point." Harold dropped his voice. "I worked at Goldenrod."

Thomas stared at him, trying to place the face but couldn't. "No, you didn't."

"Yes, I did." He nodded emphatically as if that would convince him.

"I'd know you if you were on the team. You weren't."

The boy's face flushed bright red as he sat back in the vinyl seat, the material crinkling with his movement. "You're right. I wasn't on the team, but I know the research. I know everything there is to know about the project."

Thomas didn't buy it. He narrowed his eyes in suspicion. "How?"

A nervous pulse throbbed in the kid's throat. "I can't tell you."

He huffed out a breath. "Listen, kid. I don't know who you are, or what game you're playing, but I don't have time for this. I have frozen stuff thawing in the pickup." He slid toward the edge of the seat.

"Wait."

Thomas halted on the edge of the booth. The waitress arrived and dropped the cheeseburger and milkshake, then left. He waited as the kid sat there twisting his paper napkin.

"I can help you find them and get them home." He said it so low, it was hard to hear him.

He slid back into the booth. "Explain."

"I saw William Ransom's research journals. All of them."

Narrowing his gaze, he said, "How?"

"Conner Dade turned them over to Janus Force. I read them."

He clenched his jaw. They were getting nowhere with his answers. "Again, how?"

"It's a long story I can't explain right now. I also found the research notes for the second prototype."

"I don't see how this can help me," Thomas said.

"I have an eidetic memory. And there's more you need to know, but I can't tell you here."

He stared at the kid wearing the red baseball cap with no symbol or team mascot on it. Just a plain red baseball cap. A wave a familiarity came over him as he looked at this baby-faced boy with big brown eyes and freckles on his nose. If this kid saw William's research notes and had an eidetic memory, he *did* need his help as much as he hated to admit it. He flagged down the waitress.

"Can we get this to go?" He motioned to the kid's food, then turned to him. "You're in, kid. But if you're lying to me…" He paused, unsure what threat would be terrifying enough.

"I swear on Zeus's sandals, I'm not."

Thomas paid the check while the kid packaged up his food. As they walked to the old truck, he hoped he wasn't making the biggest mistake of his life.

Chapter 1
Welcome to the Jungle

Dane startled awake. As his eyes blinked open, his first sense of his surroundings was the oppressive heat and humidity. Sweat trickled down his spine. Overhead, a thick canopy of trees filtered out the sunlight. He could hear a strange cacophony of birds, beasts and other unseen animals.

His left shoulder barked in pain. The last thing he remembered was Ark Crane showing up and opening fire. He groaned and rolled to this side, shrugging out of the oversized coat and shoving it aside.

The bullet hit him in the shoulder. Blood soaked the sleeve of the borrowed uniform. He gave it a rip and pulled it off to inspect his injury. Dark blood oozed around the entry wound. He hissed with the tenderness and knew a bullet was lodged in his shoulder.

He'd been shot plenty of times but those times, he was close to modern medicine. Glancing around, it appeared they were in a jungle or rainforest and that didn't bode well. They managed to leap from one extreme to the other.

He fumbled with the material of his ripped sleeve, trying to blot the oozing blood. He didn't have anything long enough that would serve as a bandage.

A female groan reminded him he wasn't traveling solo. He glanced around the ground foliage to see Skye's copper hair peeking out from under the bracken. He scooted closer to her. A pattern of sunlight drifted over her face as she slept, her dark lashes against her face, her lips slightly parted. Her long wavy hair was splayed out around her head, littered with leaves. One arm was out to the side, the time bender resting in her palm. He leaned over to get a look at it and saw the green display still malfunctioning with the scrambled date.

Figures.

He reached for it and tucked it into his pants pocket, wincing with the pain. He did a mental inventory of the rest of his body parts and found nothing else hurt. He was fortunate enough to land and avoid injury.

Who knew what kind of hostile natives roamed these parts? They had been lucky so far in Scotland, and then with Nyan and Ilsa. How long before their luck ran out?

Skye groaned and finally came awake. Not slowly or gently. She bolted straight up, her indigo eyes wide as she looked around and then her gaze landed on him. Relief was brief on her face before it was replaced with concern. She scooted closer to him.

"You were shot." She reached for him.

He cradled his arm to his chest and batted her hand away. "I'm shot, yes. There's nothing to do about it right now."

"We need to find a way to stop the bleeding." She looked around for something—anything—to staunch the flow. He didn't have the heart to tell her not to bother. He'd already lost a lot of blood.

"I'll be fine," he said through his teeth.

"No, you're not. You need a doctor. We have to find one."

Dane didn't answer. A doctor may be few and far between in whatever strange world they landed. He climbed to his feet, cradling his arm still, and held down his other hand to her. "We should get going. We can't stay here."

She grasped his hand and he helped haul her to her feet. She brushed away the leaves from her clothes, then shucked the heavy coat she'd worn back in winter. She dumped it on the ground in the underbrush. Then she set about getting all the leaves out of her hair. Frustration with her tangled locks was evident on her face. Her hands halted as she met his gaze.

"What?"

He hadn't realized he stared. He shook it off. She was at least ten years his junior. She was still in college and he was well beyond those years. He shouldn't have kissed her, dammit. He wasn't sure why he had.

"Nothing. Are you hurt?"

"No." She inspected her limbs, searching for cuts and scrapes, but found none. Panic flickered over her face. "The time bender—"

"Right here." He patted his pocket.

"Eventually we're going to lose that tiny thing during one of these jumps."

He didn't disagree. It was small enough it could be easily dropped. Falling though time had proved violent and knocked them both unconscious. They needed a way to stay alert during the fall, but he didn't know how to make that happen. He was no scientist.

"Let's get moving."

"Where are we going?"

"You want to sit here in the jungle for three days?"

"Not really."

"Then we need to find some place we can blend in." He eyed her hair. "Though that may be tough to do with your hair."

She ran a hand over it, pulling out more leaves and looked offended. "What about my hair?"

How could he tell her that flame-colored hair of hers was going to make her stand out like a clown at a Ted Talk?

"Never mind."

He picked his way through the underbrush, his booted feet crunching on leaves and sticks. If only he had an idea of where and when they were, that would help them. She stumbled over a fallen log. He grasped her hand in his.

"Let me help you."

~ ⧖ ~

Skye allowed him to lace his fingers with hers, acutely aware of his roughened palm against hers. Following him through the brushy path, she kept her eyes fixed on the ground so she wouldn't stumble again. At least her feet wouldn't stumble. Her heart insisted on doing that as she focused on her hand in his. Which made her think about the searing hot kiss they'd shared back in the winter time.

She didn't want to think about the kiss, but it was at the forefront of her mind. It was permanently branded there. Why had he kissed her? Sure, they'd fallen through time together a couple of times, they were stuck with one another, but she wasn't sure there was any sort of attraction there.

Oh, who was she kidding? Dane was hot. She glanced at him as he led her through the jungle, shoving aside leaves and branches for her. His looks reminded her of Clive Owen except without the accent. He was older by at least by a decade. She didn't know much about him, other than her father hired him as protection. A lot of good that did since she was the only one in her family still alive.

"Why do you suppose the hit man wants me dead?" She blurted the words before she had time to stop them from spilling out.

"Likely because you—we—have this little time machine and they want it back."

"Who's they?"

Dane halted, his feet crunching on the bracken as he turned to look at her. "You don't know?"

"Should I?"

Thoughtful consideration flickered over his features. "I guess you wouldn't."

"Do you know?" She cocked her head to the side, her eyes narrowed to suspicious slits.

"Your father told me some, but I don't know it all."

"Care to share?"

"DARPA is involved. If DARPA is involved, it can't be good."

"What's DARPA?"

His face went blank as he processed her question. "What's DARPA?" he repeated, his tone suggesting surprise.

"That's what I asked, isn't it?"

Sweat trickled down the side of his face and beaded his forehead. He released her and swiped his hand over his damp face. "Defense Advanced Research Projects Agency."

"Oh."

She still didn't have a clue. She knew her father was former military, knew he was into some top-secret stuff, but she had no idea what he did for a living.

"What do they do?"

"They're part of the Department of Defense. They develop new technologies for use by the military."

Something about the way he said it made her bristle. "You don't have to dumb it down for me. I'm not an idiot."

The implications of her father being involved with DARPA made her spine tingle and not in a good way. She understood what it meant. She understood her father was into something deep. Maybe something so deep he couldn't get out of it. That was why he had death threats. Why he was murdered. Why her mother was murdered.

"So, you understand what it means for your father to be involved with them?"

"I know he had Top Secret security clearance, if that's what you're asking." She folded her arms over her chest. The humidity suffocated her. Sweat dripped down her back. "I know his research involved things he couldn't and didn't talk about."

"Things like a mini time machine," he said.

"Things like that, yes. Did DARPA send the hit man?"

"I don't know."

She scanned the jungle around her. Had they landed in the past, present or future? It was hard to say. "Where do you think we are?"

"The jungle."

She gave him a straight face. "I know that. *When* do you think we are?"

A loud roar sounded somewhere in the distance. Gooseflesh erupted on her arms. She stepped closer to Dane. One corner of his mouth lifted in a cocky grin, lighting up the clear green depths of his eyes.

"What's the matter? Don't you like nature?"

Even though she knew he teased her, she still didn't like it. "I like nature as God intended. In a national park. Away from things that roar and can eat you."

He chuckled and took her hand again. She didn't object. As he headed through the foliage, he shoved gigantic leaves out of his way, which made them pop back in place, nearly hitting her in the face.

"Hey!" she snapped.

"Sorry."

To keep it from happening again, she held her free hand out in front of her.

As they made their way, something whizzed past his face, slicing the air between them. She peered into the brush from where it came when another and another sped by them. Dane shoved her to the ground, covering her with his body. Looking up, she saw a short spear lodged in the tree inches away from where she stood moments ago.

"I don't think we're in Kansas anymore," she whispered.

They could hear footsteps crashing through the underbrush, heading in their direction. A sudden panic welled inside her as an unfriendly someone approached. She couldn't take much more of this.

"What are we going to do?" She tried to keep her voice normal, but it wavered a little in her panic.

"Shhh. Don't move."

How could she? He sprawled on top of her, not that she minded. Her heart throbbed painfully and her breathing increased to a rapid pace. She fought the urge to squirm out from under him, but she knew he would never allow her to move.

A voice queried a question. Masculine, thick with a strange accent, speaking what sounded like Spanish…but not quite Spanish.

A response she didn't understand followed. The other voice spoke in a hushed tone.

And then, appearing before them, was a darkly tanned foot wearing a leather sandal attached to a leg with colorful beads around the ankle. She craned her neck to look up at the man who seemed taller than any other human she had ever seen. He towered over them, his head blotting out the sun and his features indiscernible.

From what Skye could tell, a richly colored material of red and gold wrapped around his hips. A long sash in the same colors crossed his hairless chest and was tossed over his left shoulder. He held a long spear, strange medallions tied around the end at the point. He looked down at them, speaking in an unfamiliar tongue.

Another man prodded Dane in the back with a spear and barked an order in his native language.

"I think he wants you to get up," Skye said. "Even though I don't want you to."

Spear Man jabbed him again.

"Stay put," he ordered and got to his feet.

Sitting up, she watched Dane stand nose-to-nose with the native, his hands in a surrendering gesture. The second native pointed his spear in her face, and spoke rapidly and firmly.

"Uh, Dane, I think this guy wants me to get up, too."

"Right," he said through gritted teeth.

The native poked her in the shoulder with the pointy spear.

"Ow! That hurt."

She rose and propped her hands on her hips, glaring at the man.

She had been right. He towered over her. His dark face was painted with white and red lines around the eyes and down the cheeks. He wore golden armbands, wristbands, a golden choker around his throat, and a large golden earring in one ear that stretched out his lobe. His eyes went wide as he sucked in a sharp breath. He fell to his knees, bowing at her feet. The other native followed.

"What the hell…?" She trailed off.

"What are they doing?" Dane glanced between the two.

"I have no idea."

"This seems like a good sign," he said. "Maybe we can use it to our advantage."

"Maybe." She placed her hand on the stranger's shoulder, gave him a light pat.

He rose, bowed his head again, then spoke to his companion. The tall one reached for Skye's hair, fingered her coppery locks between his thumb and forefinger, looking at his companion and speaking at an excited rapid pace.

"Hey, no touchy." She pushed his hand away.

Why was it everywhere they ended up, the men had to touch her? Not knowing what else to call him, she mentally named this near-giant Tall Man.

Tall Man dropped his spear, put his palms together in a prayer position and bowed to her, saying the same phrase over and over.

"Perdoe-me, ta'rin da bara. Perdoe-me."

It seemed as though he asked for her forgiveness.

"All right, all right," Skye grumbled. "I wish I knew what they were saying."

"Yeah, me too," Dane concurred. "They think you're something special, though."

"Apparently."

Tall Man picked up his spear and he and his companion urged the two of them to follow. The natives headed through the underbrush. When Skye and Dane failed to go along, Tall Man turned again, speaking to them and waving for them to come.

"I guess he wants us to follow him, eh? Do you want to see where he leads us?"

"Why not," she replied.

It wasn't the weirdest thing that had happened all day, after all.

Chapter 2
Wolf in Sheep's Clothing

They followed Tall Man and his companion through the brush along what could barely be called a path. Above, the clouds thickened and turned gray, threatening rain. She could smell the pungent twang of it in the air. The humidity pressed around them. She felt like she was suffocating.

Every few minutes, Tall Man turned to make sure they followed. When he did, he gave Skye the most riveting smile. Through the brushwood, his gait was sure footed. He knew exactly where they were headed.

The landscape changed abruptly as they left the jungle behind. They were on top of a vast mountain and now headed up a dusty path. Above them, Skye could see what looked like a village at the apex, with whitewashed buildings surrounded by grassy mountains. The air was thinner as they ascended toward their destination. Her lungs ached from the lack of oxygen and exertion.

The native people of the village gathered outside their stone huts and stared as they passed. Some had brown eyes. Others had blue eyes. They all had skin a luscious caramel color. All had dark hair. A few had sun-bleached highlights. Overall, they looked the same while she had fair freckle-spotted skin and hair the color of a shiny new penny. Maybe Dane was right about her hair. She resisted reaching up and running a hand over her locks.

The villagers whispered to one another behind their hands. Children gawked with wide-eyed wonder. Skye moved closer to Dane and grasped his hand. That quickly became second nature to her.

"I think you're a celebrity," he muttered.

"Maybe they've never seen anyone like us before."

"You've got it all wrong. They aren't looking at me. They're interested in *you*."

A wave of discomfort swept through her. She was ready for this to be over and done with. She wanted her life back, to return home.

By the time they made it through the village, they had a following. Several of the townsfolk picked up the path and walked a safe distance behind them. She couldn't help but look over her shoulder and was stunned to see how many of them were there. More joined the group the deeper into town they traveled.

Tall Man led them along the winding dusty roads, higher and higher towards the peak. The center of town hosted the largest building in the village. The sprawling round structure rose upward to the overcast sky. Behind it was a spectacular view of a snowcapped mountain in the distance and a white, foaming waterfall plunging hundreds of feet below.

As they went through town, she smelled bread baking and rich spices on the wind. Her stomach rumbled. She heard the clanging of metal and wondered if there was a smithy in one of the small buildings. Skye picked out several workers with dirt on their faces, tools in their hands. More of the villagers poked their heads out of their homes to see the two strangers. Word of their arrival traveled fast up the mountainside.

A wide stairway with hundreds of steps rose up to a yawning, dark doorway. A man in a colorful headdress stood at the top flanked by two others. Long feathers attached to the gold crown atop his head. He wore golden earrings, and several gold rings around his neck.

On his right, a woman with shiny black hair flowing over her shoulders down to her waist. She wore a sleeveless bright red tunic dress and sandals. Gold bands adorned her upper arms, wrists, neck, and ankles. On his left, a tall silver-haired man. His face was a roadmap of wrinkles and sharp blue eyes. He wore a well-worn tweed coat and brown trousers. He looked quite out of place, almost late nineteenth or early twentieth century.

At the sight of him, Skye's heart suddenly tumbled in her chest. Hope cascaded through her. Perhaps they had gotten closer to home than they had imagined. Perhaps they were in their correct time, just the incorrect place.

Dane's hand squeezed hers. His eyes were locked on the strange man in the tweed jacket.

"Do you think…?" His words drifted away.

"I'm afraid to hope," she whispered.

Hope was tempting and she wanted it very badly to be the truth. Tall Man led them up the stone stairs while the crowd waited below. She kept her eyes pinned on the trio at the top. Her legs burned more with every step. Taking the final step, they paused, Skye huffing to catch her breath. Dane wasn't even winded. Tall Man and the man in the headdress spoke rapidly.

"He must be their leader," Dane said so only she could hear.

She nodded in response, her chest still heaving. The man in the headdress turned to the man on his left and spoke something she couldn't understand. The man in the tweed coat stepped forward and gave a slight bow of his head.

"Good afternoon." He spoke perfect English with a hint of a British accent. "Welcome to Belize."

"And you are?" Dane asked.

"My name is Charles Ridgewood." He glanced from Dane to her.

Ridgewood smiled as he extended his hand to her in friendship. She took it, thinking he would shake it. Instead, he kissed the back of her hand.

"Dane Fortune, and this is Skye Ransom." Dane pushed between them. He recaptured her hand and tucked it in his elbow. Skye suppressed a smirk.

"I'm enchanted." A smile glinted in Ridgewood's bright blue eyes. "You've caused quite a stir here, milady."

"I've noticed." She peeked at the gathering crowd behind them.

"She's got a fan club, all right." Dane eyed the group, then eyed Ridgewood.

"Yes, it seems they think you are a goddess." He smiled broadly.

"Goddess?" Skye echoed.

Dane stifled a snicker. She gave him a warning glance.

"It's your hair, you see," Ridgewood replied. "They've never seen anyone with hair that color before. And I must admit it's been quite a while since I have as well."

Uneasy, Skye ran a hand over her locks, feeling the wavy, tangled strands. The leader leaned toward Ridgewood, said something in his native tongue. He motioned toward Skye first and then Dane. They both eyed his wounded shoulder.

"King Ecotzin invites you to join the royal family in a feast," Ridgewood said. "You are to be his guest of honor."

"I am?" Skye flashed the king a dazzling smile.

"He would like me to see you to the guest chambers," he said. He eyed Dane's wounded shoulder. "It appears you, sir, you're in need of a healer."

Dane nodded.

"Then I'll see you get one. I'm afraid though, Mr. Fortune, you'll have to follow behind Ms. Ransom."

This time it was Skye's turn to stifle a laugh. She hid her expression behind her hand.

"Is that so?" Dane said sourly. "Why is that?"

"They think you're her servant, naturally," Ridgewood said, as if it were an everyday occurrence. "Women are highly regarded in this culture, you see. And especially *this* woman." He motioned to her in a way that made her feel special.

"I like that." She gave Dane a brilliant grin. "I like that a lot."

"Yeah, I bet you do." He gave her a sour look.

"Come along, then." Ridgewood ushered them inside. "You must be exhausted from your travels. How did you get here?"

Skye and Dane exchanged a look.

"Uh, it's a long story," he said.

"And a bit complicated," she added.

They entered the huge building with white marble floors glossed to a high shine. The ceiling rose thirty feet high. Large iron brackets held torches illuminating the hall in bright flicking orange flame.

"Perhaps you'll regale us with the tale over the feast tonight."

"Perhaps," Dane answered.

But they both knew they couldn't tell Ridgewood the truth.

Without missing a beat, Ridgewood waved his hands to encompass the place. "This building is known as the Citadel. This is the great hall. To our right is the courtyard. We'll be dining there this evening. This way is to the royal family's private and guest chambers."

He pointed to a hallway on the left as they headed that direction. Ridgewood paused halfway down the hall in front of an oaken door with iron hinges.

"Mr. Fortune, your chamber is here. I'll send the healer shortly. Ms. Ransom, if you'll follow me."

Skye started after Ridgewood, but Dane caught her arm and pulled her to him.

"Be careful." His roughened voice whispered the words as he kept his gaze pinned on Ridgewood's back.

"Don't worry. I'm a big girl. I can take care of myself. Besides, if you're a good boy, I'll let you be my slave later." She grinned and winked at him. For a moment, she thought Dane flushed.

Ridgewood led her to the other end of the corridor and pushed open a set of double doors. Inside, the corner room exploded with color. The floor had changed from a shiny, white marble to crimson. Large, white fuzzy area rugs covered the floor by the oversized canopy bed. Gossamer curtains hung down on each side. Numerous satin pillows in red, gold, orange sprinkled the bed along with a satin coverlet. An oversized wardrobe was across from the bed. A small seating area with two chairs was next to the double windows. French doors led onto a terrace.

"Your guest suite, milady." Ridgewood said it so cheerfully, he practically sang the words.

"Wow," Skye breathed. "This is beautiful."

"Wait until you see the view."

He walked over to the French doors and pulled them open. The terrace overlooked the mountaintops, the valley below. Lush green lands and snowcapped mountain peaks greeted her. The majestic view stole her breath.

"Oh," she gasped, following him outside. The air was crisp and clean, not at all like the oppressive humidity on the jungle floor. "It's lovely."

"That it is. I'm fortunate to be a part of this place." He leaned on the handrail, the wind blowing his silver hair.

"How long have you been here?"

He gave her a small smile. "Long enough to learn their language. Tell me, Ms. Ransom, how did you and Mr. Fortune come to be here?"

She suppressed an inward cringe wondering why he lingered in her room. Why he was determined to find out the truth. He needed to go, but she didn't want to be rude and tell him to get lost.

"Shouldn't you get the healer for Dane?"

He straightened his jacket. "Quite right. He needs tending by a healer before infection sets it. Before I go, I'll show you the bathing chamber."

He led her back inside to a door next to the wardrobe. He pushed it open and motioned for her to follow. Inside, a steaming pool surrounded by terra cotta tiles. Opposite that, a sink, a crude looking toilet, a shelf stacked high with plush white towels.

Something about this place didn't mesh. These accommodations were more like a five-star resort, yet the natives appeared to possess no advanced technology or creature comforts. Ridgewood was dressed as though from another era, not of this time or place.

"There are fresh clothes in the wardrobe. I'll be along in a while to collect you for the feast. In the meantime, enjoy the facilities, relax and rest."

He gave a stiff bow before leaving her alone.

Chapter 3
Healing Magic and the Others

Dane watched Ridgewood lead Skye down the long hallway before stopping at the room at the end. When they disappeared inside, apprehension rolled through him. He wasn't sure why, but he didn't like Ridgewood. His gut gave him a warning shot. His gut was never wrong. He'd have to keep a close eye on him with Skye. He shoved open his door and stepped into his room.

It was small. A narrow bed was shoved against a wall with one window. Next to the bed, a small table. A wardrobe was across from it. A chamber pot was in one corner.

Crude and worse conditions than what they had back in wintertime. He sighed and perched on the edge of the bed, favoring his arm. A weariness he hadn't had in a long while settled in his bones. He knew most of that was from the blood loss. The bullet he'd taken for Skye was lodged in his shoulder. It was going to take surgery to get it out, something he wasn't looking forward to in this time.

A brief knock sounded on his door.

"Come in."

The door pushed open and a petite young girl stepped inside. She had wide brown eyes fringed in dark lashes, pouty red lips, high cheekbones. She wore a gold tunic dress and sandals. Her waist-length shiny black hair was swept back from her face and secured at the nape of her neck with a band of material matching her dress. She carried a ceramic bowl and had plush towels slung over one shoulder. Dane rose to his full height and realized she couldn't be more than four feet tall as he towered over her.

"Hello," he said with a nod and a smile, trying to put her at ease.

She gave him a quick curtsy and eyed his wounded shoulder. Dane sat back down and motioned her forward.

"You're here to help me?"

She nodded which indicated she understood him.

"You speak my tongue?"

Again, she nodded. She wasn't much of a conversationalist. He tried again.

"What's your name?"

She was silent another moment, then, finally said, "Tia."

"I'm Dane."

They stared at each other a long awkward moment before she moved to stand in front of him. She placed the bowl on the table next to the bed. A murky substance sloshed in it. When she eyed his shoulder again, Dane took that as a hint and removed his shirt, wincing with the searing pain in his shoulder and arm. Tia took one of the cloths off her shoulder, dipped it in the murky water. She moved close enough to him he could smell her soft scent. Her heated breath whispered over his bare skin.

"You won't hurt me," he said, trying to encourage her.

She inhaled a breath between her lips and dabbed the dried blood from his wound. She dipped the cloth again, dabbed again, until the wound was clean. She dropped the bloodied cloth on the floor and examined the wound.

"Does it not hurt?" Her voice was timid, shy.

He met her dark gaze and gave her a reassuring smile. "It hurts a little."

She reached for him then stopped. "May I?"

He gave her a nod. She placed her palm over the wound and closed her eyes. A moment later, she snatched her hand away.

"There is…something in there. A foreign object."

"Yes," he said. "A bullet."

Her brow wrinkled. "Bullet?"

"Yes, it's a…" He paused, trying to think of a simplistic way to describe it. "It's a small projectile meant to injure or kill."

"It did not kill you."

"No, it didn't."

"It was meant to kill you?"

"Yes. I was lucky, though."

"Lucky." She traced the entry wound with her fingertip. It was a delicate touch meant to soothe. "I will remove this projectile."

"Good."

He wasn't one to question, but she didn't appear to have any surgical instruments. How did she intend to remove the bullet?

His answer came when she placed her palm over the wound and closed her eyes again. Dane opened his mouth to protest but her hand started to glow. White light slashed from between her fingers. A warming sensation went through him as her hand glowed brighter and brighter.

Something moved inside him—as if the bullet itself shifted and moved through tendons and muscles. Tia pulled her hand away slowly. The light stretched from her palm to his shoulder. He could swear the bullet worked its way out of his body. She pulled her hand back more and then a wet sucking sound followed as the bullet slipped out of his shoulder. She held out her other hand and let it drop into her palm.

The light faded and winked out. Blood trickled from the wound. She stared down at the small bullet covered in blood.

"This is the…bullet?"

"Yes." He took it from her, closed his hand around it. "I'll get rid of it."

"Then I will fully heal you now."

Again, she placed her palm over his wound and closed her eyes. Her hand glowed again as she pressed against the wound. Searing pain lanced through him. He clenched his jaw, determined not to let her know how much it hurt. And then the pain was gone. She opened her eyes and removed her hand.

"You are healed," she said.

He glanced down at his shoulder. Sure enough, the wound was closed. There was nothing more than a pink scar left behind.

"How did you do that?" he asked.

"Does it not please you?"

"Oh, it does. I've never seen anyone do that before."

Tia took a step back from him and bowed her head. "It is the *mirjahall*. The healing. It is what I was born to do."

Healing magic. She was talking about healing magic. What sort of place was this he and Skye landed?

"A price will be paid," she said.

"What sort of price?" he wanted to know.

"It will be determined." She scooped up the bloodied towel and the bowl. She left before he could ask any more questions.

But a price as yet to be determined for his healing? He didn't like the sound of that one bit.

After the girl left, he couldn't resist the lure of the bed and sank into the feather mattress, drifting off to sleep.

~ ⧖ ~

Skye stood at the edge of the tub and peered down into the steaming water. When they were in wintertime, they managed to clean up and get fresh clothes. Nyan and his people had running water and working showers. This place was totally different.

A knock sounded on her door. Abandoning thoughts of a hot bath, Skye pulled open the door to see a young woman on the other side wearing a gold tunic dress and sandals. Unlike the woman on the platform when they arrived, this girl had no other adornments save for a swatch of material holding back her long flowing hair.

"Hi," Skye greeted. "Can I help you?"

"I have come to prepare you for the feast."

"You speak English?"

The girl nodded.

"How?" Skye asked.

"I learned."

When she didn't elaborate, Skye stepped aside and let her into the room. It was clear someone taught her the language. Perhaps Ridgewood himself. The girl motioned for her to follow her to the bathing chamber. She stood at the edge of the tub and pointed to it.

"You bathe. I will wash your hair."

"Oh, that's not necessary—"

"You must allow it."

Weird. Skye remained rooted in place, though, not ready to strip down in front of a strange girl.

"What's your name?"

Surprise flickered over her face. "You, too, wish to know?"

"Yes," she said, though she wasn't sure what she meant.

"Tia. And you are *ta'rin da bara*." She bowed her head low.

"Ta'rin da bara?" Skye repeated, the words feeling strange on her tongue.

The girl stepped closer and fingered her hair. "Kissed by fire. *Goddess.*" She emphasized the second syllable of the word *goddess* with the hint of her accent.

"Oh," she said, breathing the word. "I see."

"I am your servant, *ta'rin.*"

"You can call me Skye."

Her brows knitted. "Are you from the heavens? Like the others?"

Skye wasn't sure what she meant by the others, but didn't question it. Not yet. "No, Skye is my name. What I'm called." She tapped her chest. "As you are called Tia."

"It is forbidden to use your given name, *ta'rin.*"

Great. In wintertime, she was to be a sacrifice in a strange prophecy. Before that, she was to be married off to Robert the Bruce. Here, she was a goddess. What fresh hell was this?

Tia waved to the steaming tub. "You must bathe now, *ta'rin*, so we may prepare you for tonight's feast."

Skye turned her back to the girl and stripped, then quickly stepped into the hot water. She sank into the steamy tub to her chin and inhaled deeply, smelling eucalyptus in the water. Heavenly.

"Who are the others?" Skye resisted the urge to groan with pleasure as Tia scrubbed her scalp with rose-scented soap. It had been so long since she'd had any sort of luxury, this felt decadent.

The girl's fingers halted. Her voice was a shaky whisper. "It is forbidden. I should not have spoken of them."

"Do they come from the heavens?" Skye prodded.

"They come…" Her fingers scrubbed her scalp once again. "Yes, from the heavens. Only when the orb in the heavens is at its brightest."

*The orb in the heavens…*a full moon? Or did she mean the sun? What the heck kind of place was this? It all seemed so…off, but she couldn't put her finger on it. She thought back to when she and Dane talked to Thomas about the time bender in the abandoned tech building. Something Thomas said pinged through her mind.

We think because the way it bends time, it could open parallel universes.

The pit of her stomach twisted as a tingling of fear went through her. Had they somehow veered off the timeline they knew and ended up in a parallel universe? God, she hoped not. Because if that was the case, how were they supposed to get back to their own timeline in their own universe.

Tia rinsed Skye's hair and then excused herself so she could finish bathing, but all Skye could think about now was finding Dane. She had to talk to him. She sloshed out of the tub and grabbed a thick towel, drying off in a hurry, then wrapped it around her. As she entered the room, Tia waited for her holding a gold comb and a handful of ribbons in red and gold. A matching gown was laid out on the bed.

Skye perched on the edge of the bed while the girl combed out her long locks getting out all the tangles. Then she ran her hands through the damp strands until her hair was almost dry so she could work with it more easily. Skye remained as still as she could while Tia twisted her hair into a thick braid, weaving the gold and red ribbons throughout. When she was finished, she assisted in dressing her in the gown which was more like a wrap, draping it around her body in long folds. The final piece was a pair of gold sandals that wrapped all the way up her legs.

Tia turned to a nearby table and picked up a small paint brush. She waved Skye to the chair across from her. Skye eyed the brush and the pallet of what appeared to be body paint.

"What's that for?"

"For you, *ta'rin*. Please, sit."

Against her better judgement, Skye sat and watched as Tia placed red and gold markings along her shoulders and hands. When she completed the task, she held Skye by the hand and slipped a gold armband first up one arm, halting at her upper arm, and then the second arm. She slid a gold wrist band around each wrist much like the woman they'd seen on the platform when they arrived.

With her efforts complete, Tia showed Skye her reflection in a large mirror.

The material of the wrap clung to her curves, showing off her figure. Her skin had a shimmer, almost an ethereal glow. Tia had marked three lines alternating red and gold on each shoulder and the top of each hand. Each wristband had a starburst symbol on the back of them. Indicating fire?

Skye had no idea if she should thank the girl or not. As she was deciding, Tia gave her a low bow and left without another word.

Chapter 4
Offerings

Skye wasted no more time. As soon as Tia was gone, she poked her head out the door and glanced up and down the hallway. It was empty. She needed to find Dane and they needed to get the hell out of there before things got even weirder. At this point, she'd rather camp out in the jungle for the next two days than hang out in the Citadel.

She barely got two steps in when Ridgewood appeared at the other end of the hallway. A shudder of annoyance passed through her as he walked toward her, that fake smile pasted on his face. He still wore the tweed jacket, but had donned a dark blue bow tie with his khaki shirt.

"Milady, you look ravishing." He took her hand and kissed it.

"Thanks." Skye gently drew her hand away.

"Shall we join the others for the feast? I've come to escort you."

"Where's Dane?"

"I'm sure he'll join us shortly." Ridgewood stuck out his elbow.

Reluctantly, she took it. He led her past Dane's room with the closed door. Was it her imagination or did Ridgewood hurry her past? Her gut tingled with suspicion as they moved through the corridors of the Citadel. To put her mind at ease, and get more information, she struck up a conversation.

"Tell me, Mr. Ridgewood, how is it you came to be here?"

"Call me Charles, please. I insist." He flashed a smile, his blue eyes twinkling and his wrinkled face crinkling. "It's quite a story. I was a member of an archaeology exploration team several years ago. We were studying an ancient Caribbean culture known as the Nenchota."

"The Nenchota? I've never heard of them."

"I wouldn't doubt it. The Incas, Aztecs, and Mayans are more well known. At any rate, my team and I were traveling through Belize looking for evidence of their existence. A violent tribe found us first. They attacked and killed my party."

"They killed all but you?"

"I managed to escape. If it hadn't been for the Nenchota, I would not be alive today. They found me. They saved my life and brought me here."

"Why didn't you return home? I assume home is England?"

"I couldn't bear to leave them. I'd become fond of them, learned their ways, their language. They are gentle people. Kind. Resourceful. Intelligent. They've built this village over the centuries and made it thrive. They depend on no other tribes or peoples to help them."

"You sound enamored," she said.

"It's hard not to be. They're extraordinary."

"How long have you been here?"

He huffed a laugh as he thought about it. "Years. I've quite lost track. The pull of home can be great at times, though. There seems to be no cure for homesickness."

A pang of longing for her own home went through her.

"Perhaps now you'll share with me how you and Dane came to be in the jungle?"

She had no intention of telling him the truth. "We're looking for…a way home. We were shipwrecked and trying to find our way back to the coast when we were found by the men."

"I see." There was a hint of suspicion in his tone. "The coast is several miles away. Perhaps you can tell me more over the feast. Here we are."

Skye was surprised he hadn't pried more, though she suspected there was more of that to come. They exited the Citadel into a large courtyard. It was not like any she had seen. A round stone monolith rose out of the center and was surrounded by patches of green grass and stone benches. Colorful flowers bloomed along the edges of the walkways. Trees and other foliage rose up to create a serenity about the place.

On the left side of the monolith was a long table topped with numerous dishes, golden goblets and golden plates. More brightly colored flowers served as centerpieces. Candles blazed in their holders. Bamboo torches surrounded the courtyard and lit it up in a yellowish-red flickering glow.

The king and the woman from the platform sat at the center of the table. A dark-haired striking beauty was to her left. A few higher-ranking villagers mingled about, while others sat at the long table away from the king sipping from their golden goblets eyeing her as she approached the table.

"Come. You must pay your respects to the king and his family."

He paused in front of the table. He motioned to the women.

"Queen Patli and the Princess Nahuatl."

They both gave her a nod of greeting. Ridgewood spoke quickly in the strange native tongue to the king. The three royals rose and gave her a deep bow. Not knowing what else to do, she returned the bow. The king spoke to her, his dark eyes fixed on her and his hands animated.

"He says you are most welcome at his table, *ta'rin da bara.*"

Kissed by Fire.

She gave a nod to him. "Please offer my thanks to him."

Ridgewood translated and the king spoke again. Skye shifted when she realized the princess and queen stared at her. And not just the royal family. Everyone stopped what they were doing to take note of her. She wasn't fond of being the center of attention.

"He says he hopes you enjoy the feast and entertainment in your honor. But first, a tribute." Ridgewood waved to a tall chair elevated on a dais overlooking the courtyard.

She knit her brows. "I'm to sit there?"

"Aye, milady."

It took all the self-control she could muster not to stamp her foot and act like a child. She didn't want to sit there alone, elevated over the crowd as though she was something special. She scanned the crowed, but still didn't see Dane. Where was he?

The queen walked around the table to her, a smile on her lovely face as she took her by the hand. She gave her a gentle tug and walked her toward the golden chair. Skye had no choice but to follow her.

At the dais, she took the three steps up to the chair, turned and sat. As soon as she did, the royal family and the rest of the guests took their seats. Several musicians entered the courtyard. One carried a drum, another what looked like a wooden flute, another a small stringed instrument that looked much like a harp. They took up a spot next to her and started to play some of the most haunting music she had ever heard.

Servants circled the courtyard dishing food onto plates. Food that smelled divine and made her stomach growl. She watched as a whole roasted boar entered the courtyard carried by four servants who placed it in the middle of the table in front of the royals. One used a large knife to carve slabs of meat from the beast and pile it high on a plate.

Skye scanned the crowd again. Still no Dane. Ridgewood sat next to the king speaking to him. The king looked as though he held onto every word. Every now and then the king would glance her way and eye her as Ridgewood spoke. What was that man telling the king?

People rose from the table one by one and made their way to her. A little girl dropped a small bouquet of flowers at the foot of the dais. Another, a large palm leaf. A woman dropped a pillar candle, unlit. Another, a set of golden armbands she removed from her own arms. Men walked by and placed more flowers, small animals in cages—rabbits, a cat, baby chicks—at her feet. More jewels, flowers, pottery. The pile grew to a small mountain.

As everyone passed by and dropped their offerings, they gave her a low bow and called her *ta'rin*.

Someone she knew came to the dais and halted, looking up at her with those sharp green eyes and a smirk on his rugged face. Dane wore clean clothes—a rust-colored tunic and brown pants. He looked freshly shaven and clean and she spotted no sign of a bandage on his body anywhere. She blew out a breath of relief.

"Where have you been?"

"I fell asleep," Dane said. "Sorry I missed your grand entrance."

She snorted. "This was Ridgewood's idea." She looked his way. When noticed Dane, he got to his feet and hurried over to them. "Here he comes."

"Ah, Mr. Fortune. Glad you could join us." He pushed Dane aside and placed himself between the two of them. "Have you an offering for *ta'rin da bara*?"

"Who?"

"Goddess Kissed by Fire. That is the literal translation."

Dane rolled his eyes. It was Skye's turn to smirk.

"Can I get down from here now? I'm starving."

Ridgewood held his hand out to her. Dane pushed him aside as Skye got to her feet. She stepped down and grasped

Dane's hand as he led her from the chair to the long table with the royals and Ridgewood.

"I don't like this Ridgewood guy." Dane kept his voice low as he bent to talk to her.

"Me, either. And there's more I need to tell you."

"We'll talk later, *goddess kissed by fire*."

As she approached the table, everyone rose and watched her. A wave of discomfort rippled through her. Dane pulled out a chair for her. When she sat, they sat. A servant came by and placed a heaping mound of meat on her plate. Another spooned potatoes in a cream sauce next to it. Another came by and filled her goblet with wine. Skye wasted no time as she dug in.

As she started to eat, the feast continued. But the royals placed their hands in their laps and stopped eating. Ridgewood cleared his throat. She met his gaze mid-chew.

"With you at the table, *ta'rin*, the royals need your permission to continue to feast," he said.

She swallowed the chunk of meat and looked around the table at all the expectant faces staring back at her. "They have it."

The man translated to the king and the feast picked up the pace once again.

Dane regarded her with a hint of a grin. "You outrank them."

"I don't want to outrank them. I want to go home."

At the word *home*, Ridgewood cut her a glance. She ignored him while inwardly cringing.

"So do I." Dane never took his glare off him. "But we have that one small issue."

"I know." She knew, as he did, the cursed time bender had them stuck there.

"And there's more."

"Like what?" She said it around a mouthful of food. She was so ravenous she was unaware of what was happening at the table around her.

"Not here, *goddess of fire*," he mocked. She scowled and stuck out her tongue. He turned back to the table crowd and noticed Ridgewood conversing with the servant girl, Tia. "Not here. I don't trust him."

Ridgewood got to his feet, reaching for a pitcher from Tia. He poured wine from it into a goblet. They watched as he approached.

"An offering from the king. It's his special vintage." He extended the goblet to Dane.

Skye watched as he hesitated, likely considering if he should take it or not. Finally, he accepted the goblet but held it in his hand, not drinking.

"It's an insult to his majesty not to drink," Ridgewood nudged.

Dane clenched his jaw. She could see the muscles working there. With reluctance, he took a sip. Satisfied, Ridgewood returned to his seat. But something about the exchange was odd. His special vintage was for Dane and not her, the goddess kissed by fire?

"Weird," she muttered.

"I hope drinking it isn't a mistake," he said.

"I'd give my left arm for bottled water. I don't trust him, either."

"You have a feeling about him, too, eh?"

She nodded and watched the crowd of people still feasting. The music still played. The royals remained in place. As the feast wore on, Skye stifled a yawn. When could she leave the party? Or was she required to hang out all night? No one dared leave yet.

Suddenly, a light beamed from the top of the monolith. A collective gasp went through the courtyard. As the light came on and shot straight into the heavens, all those in attendance got to their feet. Skye and Dane followed suit. The villagers and the royals, even Ridgewood, moved to stand on one side of the courtyard, their faced upturned to the top of the Citadel.

"What are they looking at?" she whispered.

"That." Dane motioned upward.

She spotted it then, the oddly spaced twinkling lights hovering over the roof of the Citadel. Faint against the backdrop of night. There was no sound. Whatever hovered over it was silent, blotting out the cluster of stars. Her heart rammed into her throat as she peered up at it, her mind trying to make sense of what her eyes were seeing.

"What is that?"

He was shaking his head before she finished her question. "No idea. Never seen anything like it."

As they watched, the lights brightened to a pulsing and then lifted into the night sky and moved at a rapid pace toward the mountains. It was gone.

Skye could not shake the feeling she had just seen a UFO.

But that was impossible. Wasn't it? There was no such thing.

"That was…weird," Dane said.

"I think I saw something similar on Ancient Aliens."

Dane huffed a laugh before turning serious. "You don't think it was—"

"No. There's no way it could be a…whatever we think it is."

"I hope you're right." His eyes were still on the night sky where the thing had been.

With her heart in her throat and her nerves rattled, she nodded. She did, too.

Chapter 5
Suspicions

As the overhead lights winked out and the monolith darkened once more, everyone returned to their seats.

Except for the king. He made his exit without a word to anyone and disappeared inside the Citadel. Ridgewood sat with the remaining royals as though he belonged there and engaged in animated conversation with the queen. All the while he gave Skye surreptitious glances. She could not shake the feeling he was keeping an eye on her.

Dane reached for his goblet and took another swig. "I don't like his interest in you."

He'd noticed, too. It gave Skye a bit of comfort.

"Don't you mean in *us*? He made a subtle effort trying to pry information out of me about where we came from."

Before Dane could answer, a servant girl placed a spoonful of fruit onto their plates, then topped off Dane's drink.

"Did you tell him?" Dane's dark brows knit in concern.

"Do I look stupid to you?" When he started to reply, she put up her hand. "Don't answer that. No, I didn't tell him. He did tell me some interesting things though."

"Like what?"

"Like he's been living with them for a while."

Dane surveyed the doctor in his tweed jacket, his ridiculous bowtie, the black rimmed glasses, his thinning salt and pepper hair slicked back. Tia hovered nearby, holding the pitcher and waiting for either of them to drain their goblets.

"How did he get here?" Dane asked.

"He claims he was part of an archeological exploration and a violent tribe slaughtered his team. He was the only survivor."

"Convenient."

Dane's eyes narrowed as he peered at the man, clearly thinking the same as she. That it was suspicious Ridgewood was the lone survivor. She picked through the fruit on her plate until she found something recognizable. She sniffed, discovered a strawberry and popped it in her mouth.

"Dane, have you ever heard of the Nenchota?"

"No. Should I?"

"I haven't either. He claims they're an ancient culture and his team was searching for them."

"And?"

"And what?" She shrugged. "Not much else to tell. According to him, these people saved his life and he's been here ever since. Says he doesn't want to return home because he's happy here."

He hummed his response, still eyeing the man.

"What do you make of all that?" she asked.

"Not sure." Dane grabbed his goblet and drained the cup without as much as a wary glance into the contents.

"You're braver than I am," she remarked.

"Why? Because I drank it all?"

"Yeah." She pushed what appeared to be a mango around on her golden plate. "He seemed too interested in how we got here. Made me uneasy."

"I want you to stay away from him, Skye. I mean that."

"Hey, I can't control what other people do. He keeps popping up around my room. And this whole 'goddess of fire' thing is odd." She put air quotes around *goddess of fire* and rolled her eyes.

"Well, *I* may be popping up around your room if he doesn't leave you alone." He scowled at the man across the table.

Skye hid her smile at his choice of words. Dane's fierce protectiveness touched her.

"I'm a big girl. I can take care of myself." But she wasn't sure she meant it. She was all talk and no action.

"Is that so?" He turned his smoldering gaze on her, sending a delicious shiver up her spine. That look was similar to the one he gave her before he kissed her.

"Yes," she replied, remaining obstinate.

"If you can take care of yourself, why did I have to save you from Sovold?"

"You had to bring him up, didn't you?" She was cornered, and she knew it. "What happened there was completely beyond our control."

"Like here." He leaned close. "We don't control any of this. Not even the—" His words cut off. "You know."

She nodded. "I know."

They eyed each other with unspoken words, both knowing what the other was thinking. The time bender had cursed them, trapped them, and there was nothing to be done about it. She hated the thought of being stuck here.

Fatigue set in, making her weary. "I'm beat. When do you think I can leave?"

"Aren't you the one in charge of that?" He gave a nod to the people still lingering.

She could see a few stifling yawns and others with drooping eyes. Perhaps Dane was right. She outranked the royal family, an indication she could leave whenever she wanted.

Well, she wanted. Skye got to her feet and pinpointed Ridgewood with her gaze and announced, "I'm ready to retire. Everyone else should, too."

He translated then jumped to his feet and strode over. "Allow me to escort you back to your room."

Dane got to his feet. He reached for her arm and gave her a tug to her feet. "That's not necessary, but thanks for the offer."

He tucked her hand into his elbow and headed out of the courtyard under Ridgewood's watchful gaze. She didn't have to turn around to know he stared holes in the backs of their heads.

Dane leaned in and dropped his voice. "I think we should get out of here as soon as possible. I don't like it here."

"We have to wait for the bender to reset itself," she reminded him. "It won't work for two more days."

"I know." He exhaled a hiss. "That's what scares me."

~ ☒ ~

Ridgewood waited for Skye and Dane to disappear back inside the Citadel, a smug satisfaction oozing through him. The man was trying to protect the girl and keep her away from him. That's was fine. Before too long, the poison he put in the wine would start to work and Dane would be out cold, leaving the girl exposed.

Tia had done her job without question. She was to be commended.

She placed the pitcher on the table. "It is done, then?"

He nodded. "It is done." He reached into the inner pocket of his tweed jacket and pulled out the gold coins and dropped them in her palm with a clink. "As promised."

She looked down at the glittering coins. "Thank you, Great One."

"The others?" he asked.

"His majesty will be seeing them now, Great One."

"Good. I have business in the village. You'll let me know about our guest?"

"Yes, but…what will happen to him? Will he die?"

"That's not for you to worry about," Ridgewood said. He dismissed her with a wave of his hand.

She scooped the pitcher off the table and departed. Ridgewood stripped off the ridiculous tweed jacket and jerked off the bow tie. It was time to put his plan into action.

He left the courtyard, headed through the Citadel and exited. Down the many steps he went and walked through the village at such a brisk pace, his legs burned. It had taken numerous time travel trips to and from this place to learn about the Nenchota, to learn their language and gain their trust. What he told Skye about them had been true. They were an intelligent, gentle people.

But they were also gullible, which he knew he could exploit. Skye's flaming hair had given him all the ideas he needed. He wouldn't kill her. Not yet. She was the daughter of the late William Ransom, heir to his estate. Ridgewood hadn't been able to liquidate any of the assets because she was executor. Once he got what he wanted out of Goldenrod Research Technology, he'd shut it down. Neither DARPA nor Janus would have need of it.

As he made his way all the way through the village, with nothing more than the full moon lighting his way, he halted at the last cottage on the edge of town near the jungle. One rap on the door and he entered. Ark Crane sat in a chair by a scarred wooden table holding a flagon of wine in his hand. The light of a couple of candles flickered over his hardened face, illuminating his red-rimmed eyes.

"You're drunk."

"What else do you expect me to do while sitting here alone in this hell hole?" Ark's speech was slurred. He took another swig.

Ridgewood reached for the pitcher of wine, snatching it from the table. He tipped it upside down, letting the remaining contents splash on the dusty wood planked floor.

"I need you sober."

"Fine." Ark smacked the flagon against the table, the contents sloshing. He leaned back in the chair and propped one booted foot on the edge of the table, crossing his arms over his chest. "Your plan must be working."

"The beginning stage is, yes. In an hour or so, Dane will be out. That will be our chance."

Ark yawned. "And then what?"

Ridgewood slapped his foot off the table. It landed with a thud. "I need you to listen and understand."

The hit man sat up straight, his eyes blazing fury. "I'm listening."

"We need to separate those two. The sooner the better. Take him to the jungle. Finish him off. Dispose of the body. I don't care what you do with him. Bring me the machine if you find it on him. As soon as I can get to the girl, I'll tell her he used the time bender and left without her."

He snorted. "You think she'll believe you?"

"She won't have a choice, will she?"

"You going to kill her?"

"No, I need her alive for reasons that are none of your concern. I'll take her back with me and destroy the time machine."

Ark yawned and stretched his arms over his head. "Whatever you say, boss."

Ridgewood clenched his fists. It infuriated him the way Ark acted as though this wasn't an important mission. As soon as Dane was dead and Skye was with him, he would get rid of the hit man since his services would no longer be needed.

"Do your job and then we can go home. I've had enough of this place."

Ark gave him a two-fingered salute as he propped his foot back up on table. He folded his arms over his chest once more. "Don't worry. I know how to do my job. You do yours and stay out of my way."

Ridgewood clenched his fists, a retort bubbling inside him when he decided it wasn't worth it. He left the cottage, slamming the door behind him.

~ ⧗ ~

"What's with all the war paint?" As they left the courtyard, Dane gave her a sidelong glance at the marks Tia placed on her exposed skin.

She shrugged, acutely aware of her arm neatly tucked into his. "I have no idea what it means but I guess it has something to do with the goddess title. I noticed your shoulder is healed."

He said nothing as he made a turn through the building, a turn Skye knew was incorrect. But she went with it. She suspected he did it on purpose to keep her away from her room and thereby keeping her away from Ridgewood.

"Yes, and that's something I wanted to talk to you about. A young healer woman came to me and used healing magic. She said her native word for it, but I don't remember it." Dane stopped walking and turned to her. "She put her hand on me like this." He demonstrated by placing his palm flat on her shoulder. "Her fingers glowed. She pulled the bullet out and then healed me."

Skye stared at him, awestruck. "Are you telling me she used *magic* to heal your shoulder?"

He nodded.

She didn't want to believe him, but Dane wasn't exactly the type to make up stuff. And why would he?

"There's more. She said a price would be paid for the healing magic."

"What does that mean?"

"I don't know," he said. "I don't want to stick around to find out."

"What do you suggest? We camp out in the jungle until the time bender resets itself?"

"If we have to, yes." He took her by the arm and started walking again. "It's too dark, though. Even with the light of the full moon, I don't think we should chance it."

"That reminds me," she said. "That…*thing* we saw earlier hovering over the Citadel. Tia mentioned something about the others coming *when the orb in the heavens is at its brightest*. I can only assume she meant the full moon."

Dane halted again. "Did you say Tia?"

"Yes. Why?"

"That's the girl who healed me."

Pinpricks pierced the nape of her neck. Skye's heart lurched into her throat. "She's the one who dressed me. And she was the girl who served you all that wine."

He blanched and swallowed hard enough for his throat to bob. They stared at each other a long, silent moment.

"That's no coincidence," he finally said. "I think we should leave in the morning."

She was nodding before he finished. "I agree."

He walked her back to her room. Thankfully, Ridgewood was nowhere to be found. They paused at her door, her hand on the knob.

"You'll wake me in the morning?"

"At dawn," he said with a nod.

"Goodnight then." Still she held the knob, not opening the door. She could read the hesitation in his face.

"Are you sure you'll be all right?" The unspoken part of that was *alone with Ridgewood lurking.*

"I'm sure."

There was that spark in his eyes. That smoldering need she'd glimpsed briefly before he'd kissed her in wintertime in a situation not so dissimilar from this one. Her heart pounded a wicked beat against her chest. She could hear her ragged breathing. All she wanted in that moment was for him to kiss her again.

She didn't even know why.

Yes, she did. He was a damn good kisser.

And then it happened. He moved in, his mouth on hers in a kiss that seared through her. Her lips parted against his as his tongue tasted her, taking sips of her mouth as her head leaned against the door and his body pressed against hers. His warm, hard body. She slid her arms around his waist while his hand tangled in her hair.

She liked the way he kissed her, the way his hands fisted in her hair, the way his big body pressed against hers, making her feel small and warm and safe. She was getting way into the kissing when he jerked away from her, ripping his body from hers. Stunned, she thought for a moment she'd done something wrong when she realized he gripped his middle and hunched over with a groan.

"Dane? Are you all right?"

He fell to his hands and knees. "Help me…inside."

Skye shoved open the door and then hurried to his side. She wrapped an arm around his waist. He was bigger and stronger than her, but she managed to help him to his feet. He staggered inside her room and immediately collapsed on the floor. Sweat beaded his forehead and dampened his clothing. He groaned and curled into a ball on the floor.

She kicked the door closed and then ran to the bathing chamber, dampening a cloth and hurried back out to him. By the time she dropped to her knees next to him, he was passed out cold.

Chapter 6
Deception

Skye wiped the sweat from his forehead. Fear trickled through her. She wasn't sure what was wrong with him.

She had the distinct feeling it had something to do with the wine he drank. And Tia had been the one to give it to him.

Fury bubbled up through her. Had she been paying more attention, maybe she would have realized there was something suspicious about it.

She pressed her hand against his forehead. He was hot. Possibly running a fever. She picked up his wrist and felt his pulse. It was strong and pounding hard and fast. She hoped that was a good sign. She was no doctor. Hell, she wasn't even good at diagnosing her own illnesses. What was she supposed to do now? She knew she couldn't heft him up on the bed. He was too heavy.

Heaving a sigh, she sat on the cold tile floor next to him, leaning against the wall. She grasped his hand. Holding it gave her comfort. Not that he knew she was there. He didn't. Despite the wide yawn, she was determined to keep a vigil and make sure he was okay. But her eyelids were awfully heavy and she wasn't sure she could keep them open. She was…so…tired.

It wasn't long before she drifted to sleep with her head against the wall and her hand still in his.

~ ⧖ ~

The soft snick of the door closing was enough to make Skye's eyes pop open. Sometime during the night, the candles had burned down to nothing and snuffed out. The suite was plunged into darkness. Dane's body was still curled on the floor next to her. She still held his hand. And standing at the door was a shadow figure peering down at both of them.

A cold chill skirted through her as she realized there was an intruder in her room. Skye shuttered her eyes so she could peer through her lashes as she watched the lithe figure swing open the door, the slash of light from the hallway illuminating the slender women for a brief moment before she moved with fluid grace. A moment later, she returned followed by a tall hulking man.

A form she knew.

A face she recognized.

Ark Crane.

He'd followed them through time again. What disturbed her even more was Tia helping him. Why was she helping him? What did she hope to gain?

Her fear spiked. What was she going to do? What *could* she do? She couldn't fight Ark Crane. He was a trained killer and she was a…a nothing. She had zero skills. Her heart rammed hard in her chest, the throbbing so painful she thought it might burst through skin and bone.

He stood over them, looking down at Dane, ignoring her. When he noticed her hand still in Dane's, he snorted as if it was the stupidest thing he'd seen all day. Tia stood in the doorway, glancing every so often over her shoulder.

"He comes," she whispered then.

A second later Ridgewood was in the room. What was happening?

The two of them hoisted Dane up between them, one on each side of him. Oh, no. No, no, no. They were taking him away, separating the two of them. Likely that had been the plan all along. Her pulse thrummed in her ears as she tried to decide what to do. She didn't have the strength to stop them. Ridgewood, or Ark Crane, could easily overpower her if she protested. She needed to stay still and quiet and figure out a way to get to Dane and rescue him.

They slipped out of the room. Tia closed the door quietly behind her, leaving Skye bereft and alone.

The hit man and Ridgewood were working together. The realization of it hit her like a punch in the gut. She and Dane were right in that they both suspected Ridgewood was not who he appeared to be. There were so many questions circling her mind. How did they know each other? Was Ridgewood a hit man, too? Was he from her future as well?

She peeled her tired, cold body off the floor and went to the door. Cracking it, she eyed the empty hallway before pulling the door open the rest of the way. She took one step into the hallway and stopped.

There was no one about. Ridgewood and Ark Crane had taken Dane away in a hurry.

And, she realized with some horror, he still had the time bender.

~ ⧗ ~

Skye paced the length of her suite, trying to decide what to do. She had no weapon, not that she'd know how to use one. She had no combat or self-defense skills whatsoever. Even if she confronted Ark and Ridgewood, she didn't know how to handle them. She didn't know what she could do. Nor did she have a clue as to where they took Dane. She didn't know her way around the palace except to and from the courtyard.

Thinking of Ridgewood sent fury through her. All this time, he was working with the hit man who had been sent to kill her. She knew she had a bad feeling about Ridgewood from the start. Her gut had been right.

Her gut had also been right about the wine Dane had. And Tia helped. Her hands clenched. If she saw that girl again, she'd give her a piece of her mind.

Clearly, they both thought she had been asleep when they came to get Dane. Why take him and not her, too? Unless they were trying to separate them. She didn't like the thought of that either.

Dawn broke through the windows of the doors to the terrace. She'd been up all night trying to figure out what to do. She still had no answers.

The door knob jiggled and she halted her pacing, her heart in her throat. She looked around for a weapon and snagged a nearby vase, ready to toss it at whoever entered her room. The door cracked open and the dark-haired Tia entered.

"Tia." Skye said her name on a sigh of relief. And then the anger overcame her. She replaced the vase in a hurry. It wobbled on the base before settling but Skye was too mad to notice as she charged toward the girl.

"I've come to prepare you for the day—"

Before she could finish, Skye wrapped her hand around her upper arm, her fingers digging into the girl's delicate flesh. Her eyes flew wide as she looked up at her.

"*Ta'rin*…you're hurting me."

"Good." Skye kicked her door closed, then dragged Tia toward the terrace. She flung open the door. "You're going to tell me everything you know about Ridgewood."

Skye wasn't thinking clearly as she shoved the girl out onto the terrace and pushed her against the railing. With one hand on her upper arm, she wrapped her other around the girl's throat.

"Everything," Skye repeated. "Or I will crush your windpipe."

Tia's bottom lip quivered. No, no, no. That's not what she meant to say.

"*Ta'rin*, I am sorry. I had to help the Great One."

"Great one?" She snorted. "Ridgewood, you mean."

The girl nodded.

"Where did they take Dane and why?"

"I do not know." When Skye's fingers dug into her throat she gasped. "It is the truth."

She relaxed her hand. If the girl truly believed Ridgewood was the Great One and she was the Goddess of Fire, perhaps it was time to leverage her title a bit.

"You betrayed me," Skye said.

Tears welled in the girl's eyes. She bowed her head. "I did."

"Why?"

"The Great One told me if I did not help him, he would kill me. If I did help him, he would give me these." She reached into her pocket and held up a palmful of gold coins.

Skye stared at them a long moment. "You betrayed me for gold."

Fat tears streaked down her cheeks. "I need the gold for passage on a ship."

"A ship? Why? You're leaving?"

She nodded. "I do not belong here. On my sixth year, I was stolen from my mother's arms by the Akota and enslaved."

"Who are the Akota?"

"They are a war tribe."

Horror flickered through her. This young, beautiful girl had been stolen and enslaved and who knew what else happened to her. She could only guess the horrible things that had happened to Tia as a slave of the Akota. She didn't understand how people could treat others that way.

Ridgewood's story about his team members dying came back to her. It was clear he had taken true bits and pieces of this world for his own use and exploited it. He brainwashed

Tia and likely the royal family he was someone powerful and special, like he indicated Skye was.

"I'm sorry," she said.

"It is the way of things."

"How did you end up here with the Nenchota?"

"I escaped when I was two-and-ten and found my way here. They took me in, elevated me as a handmaiden for the queen and princess. I have them to thank for my well-being these last few years, but I long to go home. I do not know if my mother still lives."

A pang stabbed Skye's heart. She released her and stepped away, running her hand through her hair. Standing at the railing, Skye stared at the beautiful scenery beyond. There were still things she didn't and couldn't understand, but at least she knew more about Tia. A girl who was looking out for herself and no one else. She couldn't fault her for that.

Still, it didn't answer her question about Dane. She had to find him. The sooner the better. Their time bender window was approaching. She wasn't sure what would happen if they missed it. Would the bender still work? Would they be able to time jump?

"I have to find my friend," she said.

"I cannot help you," Tia said.

"Why not?"

"If the Great One learns I helped you, he will kill me."

There was true fear in her eyes. "He won't. My friend and I will protect you. I promise you that."

There was one thing she knew for certain and that was Dane would never let Ridgewood harm her, or anyone else. And neither would she. Skye didn't know where to start looking. She turned to the girl, this time reaching for her hand.

"If you can help me, I'll make sure you get to that ship," Skye said "We both will. But I have to find him and the only way I'm going to do that is if you help me. I need to know where the Great One spends his time. You *must* know."

Her face paled, giving her a sickly pallor behind her caramel complexion. Tears still welled in her eyes, but at last she nodded. Skye squeezed her hand and gave her a smile.

"Good, then, let's get started."

Chapter 7
Secrets

Dane woke with a raging headache. The first thing he noticed was his wrists were bound behind him. The second thing he noticed was he was on a dirty wood-planked floor. It took several seconds for him to realize he was no longer in Skye's palatial suite. It took some effort, but he managed to push himself to a sitting position.

Now that he was upright, he could tell he was in a small house. Likely one that was in the village and not in the Citadel. A table stood in the center. A crude kitchen was beyond. Dane scooted himself back against one of the walls and leaned against it and peered around. On the other side of the house, a narrow bed was shoved against the wall. There was a curtained alcove that he assumed was the bathroom.

He took a deep breath and cleared his fuzzy mind, trying to remember what happened. The last thing he recalled was kissing Skye. Damn it all. He had succumbed to kissing her again. He closed his eyes and thumped his head against the wall, as if that would clear away the memory. It didn't. He'd done it, not once, but twice now. Neither of them had spoken of it. But she'd been giving him those fluttering eyelashes since they landed here.

Seeing her with all that war paint all over her exposed skin did something to him. She *did* look like a Goddess of Fire in that tunic dress. It hung in elaborate folds that clung to all her curves.

Again, he thumped his head against the wall. He had to stop thinking about Skye like that. He'd made a promise to William Ransom to keep her safe. He intended to uphold that promise. Kissing her and thinking about her in ways he shouldn't wasn't part of the deal.

When he scrubbed *that* memory away, he remembered *why* he stopped kissing her. He was gripped with horrific stomach pain. He couldn't stay conscious and passed out. The only way he could have ended up here was if he was moved by someone bigger and stronger than Skye. That someone had to be Ridgewood.

He should have stayed away from that wine. He should have listened to her and his gut instincts. He knew Ridgewood was shady, and yet he allowed himself to become the victim. Now, Skye was separated from him, leaving her alone and exposed. He had to get back to her. He twisted his wrists together, trying to feel for the knot. As he did so, the rope cut into his flesh. He got a burning sensation for his trouble.

The front door opened, a slash of morning light coming into the small house. The silhouette against the sunlight was a hulking man. One he recognized.

Hot sweat broke out on the back of his neck.

The door slammed closed. It took several moments for Dane's eyes to adjust but his instinct was right on. Ark Crane stood before him, staring him down with cold, desolate eyes. Dane stilled his hands and stared back at him.

"Surprised to see me?" Ark finally asked.

"No." Despite his immediate response, he *was* surprised to see the man in their time zone. Ridgewood and Ark in the same place and time could not be good for him or Skye.

"Do you know why you're here?"

"I can guess," Dane said.

"And you'd be right."

"Where is she?" He didn't think it was necessary to clarify he meant Skye.

"Does it matter?"

"Yes." His heart leapt into his throat. If Ridgewood did anything to her, he would rip the man into tiny pieces.

Ark gave him a faint grin. "She's in good hands. Don't worry."

"Ridgewood's." Dane didn't bother to hide the sour note in his voice.

"He's taking her back."

"Back?" Warning bells went off in his head.

"Home."

Home. The pulse in his wrists pounded hard against the ropes as he stared up at the hit man. "No," Dane said, his tone flat.

"You don't get a say."

No way was she leaving with Ridgewood. Why did he want her? What sort of ugly plans did he have for her? Who *was* this Ridgewood guy? And how did those two end up working together? Had Ridgewood hired the hit man?

Too many questions and not enough answers.

He tried to get out of his ropes hoping Ark wouldn't notice the way he twisted and turned his hands to and fro. The rope burned through his flesh, shredding it. It wasn't long before his wrists were slick with blood and sweat.

"If he hurts her, I'll kill him."

"Is that a threat?" Ark asked.

"No, a promise," Dane replied.

"I can't see the man keeping her alive much longer. At least not until he gets what he wants," Ark said. "But you'll already be dead, so you won't care." He pulled a menacing-looking knife from a sheath at the small of his back.

That's the way it was to be, then. "You're going to kill me without giving me a chance to defend myself?"

"Yes, because I need you dead." He reached into his pocket and brought out the time bender. "And I needed this. So, thank you for making it easy."

Dane stared at the small device in his hand and knew he had been a fool to think keeping it on him was the safest idea. He should have given it to Skye and had her hide it in her suite. Now, the faulty time bender—their only way out of his hell hole—was in the hands of his enemy.

And so was Skye.

Ark pocketed the device and advanced. He reached for him, grabbing a fistful of his tunic and yanking him upward. It took several seconds for Dane to get his feet under him but he finally managed to stand. All the while loosening the ropes and ignoring the burning pain.

Ark stepped back, holding up the knife looking as though he'd won a great victory. Hesitating long enough for Dane to get his bearings. As the hit man lunged, Dane freed his wrists in time to block his first attack with his forearm. He grabbed the wrist of Ark's knife-wielding hand holding it out of the way so he could punch him. Ark's head snapped back, his jaw clicking with a sickening snap.

All that did was anger him further. He lunged again. Dane blocked again. Kneed him in the groin. Ark grunted and bent over enough for Dane to knock the knife out of his hand. It clattered to the floor. With a frustrated growl, Ark barreled into Dane's mid-section, shoving him back against the wall.

Dane stomped on his toes then elbowed him in the face. He stumbled back, blood forming at the corner of his mouth and dripping from his nose. With him momentarily stunned, Dane dove for the knife, snatching it up.

Ark tackled him against the floor, grasping his wrist and slamming it against the floor to get him to release the knife. Dane tightened his grip and elbowed him in the gut. He grunted and rolled off him. Dane got back to his feet as Ark lunged for him again.

Dane stabbed him in the side hard enough to hurt, but not hard enough to kill him. He intentionally missed an artery. He pulled out the knife and dropped it. He reached into the hit man's pocket and recovered the time bender, then gave him a shove backward. The hit man stumbled away, swiping his hand through the blood on his side.

"You have about twenty minutes before you bleed out," Dane said. "I suggest you find yourself a healer."

He left the house. His only thought was getting to Skye.

~ ⧗ ~

Skye pulled open the door of her suite and peered into the hallway. It was deserted. She motioned for Tia to follow her. They stepped into the drafty hallway and for the first time, she noticed torches flicking in brackets along the white marble walls. Why had she only now noticed that?

With quick, light steps, Tia took the lead and hurried down the corridor. The girl could move fast. Skye had a hard time keeping up with her. She hoped finding Ridgewood would help her find Dane. Only the fear of being stuck here indefinitely kept her going, kept her spurred into action.

The drafty passage left her with an eerie feeling. As she hurried behind Tia, someone barreled into her, slamming her against the opposite wall. The surprise attack forced a high-pitched yelp from her.

Before she could regain her footing, a steely hand clamped over her mouth, another wrapped around her waist. Her head exploded as a blunt object struck the back of her head. It was the first time in her life she saw stars, blurred her vision. The last thing she saw before passing out was Tia's fear-stricken face.

~ ⧗ ~

Skye came to and found her arms shackled to a wall and her mouth gagged. Her head throbbed with pain. It was difficult to make her eyes focus on her surroundings. She blinked several times.

She was in a dungeon with cold, damp air pressing in on her. Through the cell door, orange-red flames flickered from a line of torches. The blazing fires were the only sound she could hear in the deathly silence. That and her soft whimpering.

Footsteps shattered the quiet and long shadows wavered along the wall as Ridgewood entered. Two men followed him. A key clanked in the lock and the door swung open with a creak.

"I see you've come around." Ridgewood handed the key to one of his lackeys. One held a torch, illuminating that small dank cell.

She squinted in the darkness—as if that would help— trying to see his face. The firelight did nothing but cast his features in hideous shadows.

"Now that we've rid you of your bodyguard, we can discuss the truth." He stepped close in the pale light and removed her gag.

Skye tilted her head back, looking down her nose. "What truth?"

He produced the time bender from his pocket and turned it end over end. Her heart lurched as she looked at the small device in his hand. That's why he was after them? Because of the time bender? If he had it, then Dane was…no, she refused to believe Dane was dead.

"What is that?" It was difficult to keep her voice steady with a hint of curiosity. She knew what he held.

"Come now. What sort of fool do you take me for? This is a brilliant little machine, isn't it?"

He turned it end over end and held it up for her to see. She got a good look at it. Relief sputtered through her as she realized his was different from their time bender. It was bigger than her version, but yet she could clearly see the black button and the digital read-out. Hers was the length of a lipstick, while his was the size of a pen. How did he have one, too? Why? Where was Thomas? Did he help Ridgewood build it?

"Who are you really? Is your name even Ridgewood?"

"That, at least, is true." His wrinkled face crinkled with his smile. "The rest I told you was using my powers of persuasion."

"Your powers of persuasion? Don't you mean a lie?"

"No. It's true the Nenchota trust me."

"Yes, Great One, so I've heard."

He didn't bother to hide his pleasure at that. "It was necessary to gain their trust. To make them think of me as a prophet."

She snorted. "That's hilarious. You, a prophet?"

"Why do you think you were named Goddess of Fire? I prophesied you were coming. Your arrival proved me right."

A hot tingling sensation prickled the back of her neck. Somehow Ridgewood knew they were going to time travel there. The only way he would know that was if he had access to her father's lab. The only way he would have access to her father's lab was if Conner and the others allowed it to happen. She didn't even know if Conner was still alive. All she remembered was Lucy, who was also on her father's team, had tried to kidnap them, too.

Everyone was after the little time bender, it seemed. But how much of a hot commodity could it be with a second one in play? She stared at the device in Ridgewood's hand, her stomach cramping. It made sense. The second one allowed Ark Crane to follow them into wintertime. He time leapt after them and when he missed his shot, he must have returned to their present.

But it didn't answer the question as to who Ridgewood was or how he got his hands on the time bender. Or even how Ark Crane had arrived here, too.

"Who are you?" she demanded.

He enclosed the device in his hand and paced the small confines of the cell. "I've spent quite a lot of time here coming and going. The Nenchota taught me a lot. Their language. Their culture. Their strengths. Their weaknesses." He halted and gave her a glance. "That they still believe in deities and worship them. That's why they worshipped you. It took me months to earn their trust. They are a cautious people. Once I did, I knew I could plant the seed of your arrival since I knew when and where you and your bodyguard would land. I knew I had to elevate you to get the help of the servant girl and the royal family."

"You tracked us?"

He nodded.

Ridgewood was smarter than she realized. He had crafted the deception of her identity with ease. He'd somehow made these people believe he was all-knowing. He'd spent a fair amount of time with them using the time bender on more than one occasion to travel back and forth. Which meant his device could get them home.

She eyed it, wondering how to get it away from him.

"And what time period is this?" she asked.

"That is the most interesting part. This time is not on any calendar we are familiar with. Funny thing about this device." He held it up, looking at the digital read-out. Besides the usual date, it had another set of numbers she couldn't make out. "It can break through parallel universes."

She wanted to laugh. She really did. But she knew he was telling the truth. She remembered what Thomas Hardy said that day in the old tech building—the time bender could do just that.

Oh, God. The only brainiac she knew that could help him track her and Dane was Thomas Hardy. Where was he? Was he somewhere safe? Was he forced to work with this lunatic?

"How well do you know your father?" He abruptly changed the subject.

She was taken aback by the question. "He was my father. I knew him well enough." Maybe she didn't know he had built a time machine, but she knew *him*, loved him, respected him. He raised her with integrity and solid morals.

"He wasn't such a saint, you know. He planned to sell this little invention to China for millions. Billions maybe. I'm not quite sure."

Skye's heart plummeted to her churning stomach. Her father would never—could never—do such a thing. William Ransom was a patriot and a fiercely loyal one. He had once served in the armed forces and then moved on to working with the Department of Defense. He was well-respected in his circles. A traitor he was not. Surely there was another explanation.

"I don't believe you," she said, her voice a faint whisper.

"I wish it weren't true, my dear. He had plans to have it mass produced."

"My father would never sell out his country for money, no matter how much it was."

"I'm afraid it is true." He gave her a thin-lipped smile that didn't quite reach his eyes. It left her feeling cold. "Your father would have done anything to keep his wife alive. *Anything.*"

Even sell out to the Chinese? No. She couldn't and wouldn't believe he would stoop to such measures. She shook her head.

"Your mother, Skye, had stage four bladder cancer. He knew she was going to die and yet he was going to do whatever it took to keep her alive. Even mass-producing this" —he shook the time bender— "as a means to save her life and pay the mounting doctor bills."

She stared at him, a cold prickly sensation moving up her spine and into the back of her throat. It *was* true there were a lot of doctor and hospital bills she'd had to contend with after her parent's murder. The only saving grace had been the life insurance policies on both of them that had helped pay most of them off in addition to burying her parents. The sting of tears pricked her eyes as she thought of all that again. She hated him for dredging up those memories.

"You're lying."

"No," he said, matter-of-factly. "You know I speak the truth. However, I suspected you wouldn't believe me. I have proof."

"Then let me see it."

"I cannot show you here. You're coming with me."

She stared at him in disbelief. "I am not. Besides, even if you take me with you, Dane can still follow you." She said it with a bit of hope that their time bender would actually send him back home.

He smirked, amused at her thought process. "I'm afraid that won't be possible, my dear. You and I both know your time bender is faulty, whereas mine is not. Aside from that your traveling companion has already left without you."

Her eyes pricked with sudden hot tears. She was certain the bender had not reset itself. She was also certain Dane wouldn't leave her behind. Not after those kisses.

"No. I saw you."

He lifted an eyebrow in question. "You saw me?"

"Yes, you and your henchman. The two of you came into my room and took Dane away." She lunged for him, rattling the chains on her wrists. The iron manacles cut into her skin. "Where is he?"

"It's unfortunate you saw that. The girl assured me you were sleeping. Pity I will have to punish her for that."

"You leave Tia alone." Skye said it with such vehemence, she almost didn't recognize her own voice.

He sighed. "You're coming with me. I have a few arrangements to make before we depart."

"I'd rather *die* than go with you." She spit in his face

Angered now, he backhanded her across the mouth with his enclosed hand, jarring her jaw. The blow surprised her, stung her, and left it throbbing with pain.

"I don't need you in one piece to return, but I *do* need you. We have some loose ends to tidy up."

"Where is Dane?"

"You really have to know, don't you? All right, then. Your bodyguard will not be joining us or riding to you rescue this time because he's dead."

More lies? Or could this be the truth?

Ark Crane was here. Ark Crane was the man hired by Conner to kill her. Hot tears pricked her eyes. She didn't want to believe it.

"It is the truth, my dear. I'm sorry."

"Go to hell," she spat.

"Perhaps I will when all of this is over. We leave soon."

The men left her alone in the cell, the door slammed shut behind them with a finality she didn't want to think about. After their receding footsteps, the only sound was that of her whimpering. If Dane was dead, then she was on her own.

She didn't like that one bit.

Chapter 8
Curse of the Others

Skye drifted in and out of sleep, her head hanging between her shoulders. Ridgewood had left her there in the dank cell. She knew he would return eventually to make good on his threat to take her back with him. She didn't want to go. As much as she wanted to get back home, it was not under those circumstances.

A key clinked in the lock. The cell door swung open with a groan and a squeak. And then there was silence. She didn't hear even a footfall which she thought odd. Ridgewood would have made a little noise and likely he would have come with others.

She lifted her head and stared into Tia's wide fear-rimmed eyes. She stood in the cell doorway. "Tia, what are you doing here?"

The girl held up the ring of keys. She stepped deeper into the cell. As she neared, Skye could see her pale tear-streaked face. Her hands shook as she unlocked her wrists.

"You shouldn't be here," Skype said. "Ridgewood thinks you betrayed him."

The girl didn't respond as she unlocked her other wrist. Skye dropped her arms, the blood rushing back into them making her skin prick with hot, painful needles. Tia dropped the ring of keys on the floor with a *thunk* and motioned for her to follow. When the girl turned, Skye gasped.

Tia's back was shredded. She'd been whipped.

"Tia," Skye whispered.

"It will heal."

But Skye could see the shiny blood as it clotted along each lash on her skin. She put a hand on the girl's arm and halted her.

"He did this to you?"

She nodded. "He was right to."

Horror shuddered through her. How *could* he? She was nothing but a young girl trying to make the best choices she could in an unfair world. He had no right to use her like that. No right to beat her. Fury pounded through her.

"No, he wasn't. What happened wasn't your fault. You need a healer."

Tia shrugged off her hand. "I will be fine. Come."

"Tia—"

"There is no time. *Come.*"

Withing waiting for a response, the girl exited the cell and headed through the dungeon. Skye followed, hurrying to keep up with the girl's quick steps.

"Where are we going?" she asked.

"There is a tunnel under the palace. It will take you outside the village. Only a few know of it. You will be able to escape."

"I'm not leaving here without my friend."

Tia stopped so quickly Skye nearly ran into her. The girl turned to her, sadness deep in her eyes. She looked as though she wanted to say something but couldn't find the words.

"What is it?" Skye prompted.

"The man was taken away to be killed." She pressed her fingers against her quivering lips.

Skye's heart quickened, throbbing with a pain she had never before felt. Ridgewood's threat wasn't a threat after all. It was the truth. Dane had been drugged and taken away. Perhaps Ark Crane needed him incapacitated to kill him.

"You know this for certain?"

Tia nodded.

Skye sagged against the wall. It was impossible to stop tears from burning her eyes. Dane was her anchor, the only one keeping her sane on this journey. Without him, she would be lost and alone. She wanted to fall apart at the seams, but she knew she couldn't do that. Not here. Not now. She had to remain strong. And she hated that. She had been strong when her parents were killed. She hadn't allowed herself to break down like she wanted to so many times. Like she wanted to now.

Perhaps she was cursed. It seemed the people who got closest to her died.

"I must take you to the tunnel."

"No," Skye said. "It doesn't matter."

"Escape is all that matters, *ta'rin*."

"No," Skye insisted.

Dane had the time bender when he was taken away. Likely it was in the hands of Ark Crane by now. It would do her no good to escape. Where would she go? At this point she'd be better off going with Ridgewood.

"But—"

"You don't understand," Skye said. "Without Dane, it doesn't matter now."

She couldn't look at Tia's stricken face. There was no point in trying to explain why she didn't need to escape. It would be too complicated.

"You should take me to the Great One," Skye said. "Or take me back to the cell before I'm missed, and you get in more trouble."

"I will not take you back there or to him." Tia shook her head, her words firm. "He is no great one."

That, at least, was the truth. Skye was glad to see the girl had a backbone at least. "And I'm no Goddess of Fire. That was a lie he told you."

Tia reached for her hands and gripped them. "Please, *ta'rin*. You must to go the tunnel with me. I beg you."

She sighed. "And go where? There is nothing for me here."

She could see the girl's mind working as she thought of some reason for Skye to stay, some place to go. She squeezed her hands. "Come with me."

Skye was so taken aback by that she didn't know what to say. She gaped at the girl.

"My mother will be very glad to have you. Please, *ta'rin*. I cannot leave you here."

God, wasn't that the sweetest thing she'd ever heard? Hot tears prickled the backs of her eyes. She wanted to hug the girl but refrained due to the lashes on her back.

"But you said you only have enough gold for one to buy passage on the ship."

Tia looked at her red hair. "You are Goddess of Fire. They will give you passage for free."

The girl was serious. There wasn't a hint of a smile on her face anywhere. Skye couldn't believe she would invite her to her homeland. She hardly knew the girl. She chewed her bottom lip, considering. She could stay and go back with Ridgewood, yes. But why? What was left for her there? Her parents were gone. She doubted she still had any credibility left with her college professors due to her lengthy absence. She had no boyfriend waiting for or wondering if she were even still alive.

"All right. I'll come with you."

A smile of relief broke on Tia's face. Taking her by the hand, she led her down the hallway with the flickering torches. She didn't know why she said yes, but it made Tia happy. They left the dungeon and took the steps upward. Skye never looked back.

~ 𝄞 ~

The main road in the village was a bustle of activity as Dane pushed and shoved his way up the slope trying to get back to the Citadel. All he could think about was getting to Skye and finding her. He hadn't made it very far when he could hear shouts behind him. He halted when two men who were dressed as village guards stepped in front of him, crossing their spears to keep him from passing.

The commotion escalated into a cacophony behind him. He turned to see Ark Crane stumbling up the road holding a hand against his bleeding side. His shirt had a large wet red stain. Blood seeped between his fingers.

He was determined, wasn't he?

Ark barked one word in the native language. It caught Dane by surprise. He halted and gave the man a look over his shoulder. Guards pressed around him, their spears pointing at him. He knew Ark was after the small device he had in his pocket. The hit man would have to kill him to get it back.

Today was not a good day to die.

He planned to walk away from here, find Skye, and get the hell out of here. The time bender had almost reset itself.

"I called you a thief." He gave him a wolfish grin.

"I'm no thief," Dane replied.

"I'm glad Ridgewood taught me their language. I'm going to make sure they understand who you are and what you did."

Ark spoke again in their tongue and held up his bloodied hand.

"I told them you stabbed me and tried to kill me."

Dane shifted from one foot to the other, deciding how to react. The guards glanced from Ark back to him when he noticed murmurs going through the crowd. The villagers moved closer. A few of the faces he recognized from the previous night's feast.

"You aren't one of them," Dane said at last. "You're nothing."

Sweat beaded Ark's forehead and slipped down the side of his face. Dane knew if he didn't have that stab wound tended soon, he'd die. He tried to show him some mercy by allowing him to live, even though the man shot him, kidnapped him, stole the time bender, and tried to kill him a second time.

Ark spoke again to one of the guards. Then, to Dane, "I asked them to arrest you."

"*Pardeo.*"

A man he couldn't see spoke. He weaved his way through the villagers and finally exited the crowd. He halted in the open space between Ark and Dane. He was tall, dressed in a silk tunic in burnt orange, dark brown pants and soft shoes. The clothes of a nobleman. He had a high forehead, a thin straight nose and full lips. Dane recognized him as one of the nobles from the feast. He spoke again in the native language. The only words Dane understood were *ta'rin da bara.* Whatever he said infuriated Ark. His face turned bright red. A collective gasp went through the crowd. Ark narrowed his eyes and glared at them both.

Even though she wasn't here, Skye saved his hide.

The man turned to Dane. "I told them not to harm you. That you are the servant to *ta'rin da bara.*"

"You speak English?" Dane asked.

"The Great One taught a few of us. He did not teach the commoners."

Dane bit off the laugh that wanted to erupt. Is that what Ridgewood was calling himself here?

The man's gaze cut over to Ark. "You. Who are you? I have not seen you here before in our village. You are a stranger."

Dane suppressed the smile that wanted to tug at the corner of his mouth. Ark glared daggers at the nobleman.

"A visitor, perhaps," Dane suggested, then nodded at his bloodied tunic. "He needs a healer. He had an accident with a knife."

The nobleman met Dane's eyes. "And why should we heal him?"

Dane considered. Why should they heal him? He wasn't exactly a standup citizen. He killed people for money, after all. But like him and Skye, Ark didn't deserve to die in a place that wasn't his home.

"He's far from home. Heal him so he can make it back there."

The nobleman was silent a long moment and then at last gave a nod. "Very well. My personal healer will tend him." He jerked his head in a nod to one of the men standing nearby. They hurried to Ark's side. The hit man had no choice but to follow him.

Dane didn't particularly care if the hit man got out of this time or not. His first and only concern at the moment was finding Skye.

"I have to get back to the Citadel," Dane said.

He didn't wait for a reply as he started back up the slope. The man followed.

"I will escort you."

"That's not necessary," Dane said.

"I must insist," the nobleman said.

Dane cringed. Fine, then. They fell in step together. "Tell me more about this Great one."

"The Great One taught many things. We learned to communicate with either other by teaching our languages to the other. He is the one who prophesied the coming of *ta'rin da bara*."

He clenched his jaw, hard. This is what Ridgewood was doing? Prophesizing to these innocent, naïve people about the arrival of a goddess? How long had the man been here? How much forethought, planning, and groundwork did he do to prepare them for their arrival?

"He did not mention she would have a servant, though."

"We're a package deal," Dane said. "Where she goes, I go."

"Then why are you not with her now?"

"We got separated." Dane didn't think it necessary to explain it was by force.

"Will she be able to release us?"

Dane halted in the middle of the street. What an odd question. "What do you mean by that?"

"We made offerings to her at the feast. Offerings that would help release us from…" He paused, glanced around to see if anyone listened. When he saw several villagers staring them down, he took Dane by the arm and resumed walking. He dropped his voice low and leaned closer. "From the curse."

"What curse?"

"The curse of the Others."

Dane knit his brows. "Who are the Others?"

"Your pardon, sir, but we cannot speak of it here." He waved his hand to encompass the open road of the village. "We will speak more once we reach the Citadel. I will request an audience with his majesty."

"For what purpose?"

"We will discuss it then."

Dane didn't like where this was going. He hadn't realized there was some significance to the offerings she received at the feast the night before but it was clear now there was something to it. Something this nobleman and these villagers' thought would help break this curse—whatever it was.

He had a very bad feeling about this.

Chapter 9
Tunnel to Escape

Dane and the nobleman arrived at the Citadel and ascended the steps. The man led him through the shiny marble halls to two wooden double doors. He pushed them open and led him into what could only be the throne room. The floors changed here from the white marble to solid black and a soaring ceiling so high, Dane could barely make it out. The inky blackness was only separated by twinkles of light mimicking the night sky. Ahead of them, two wooden chairs which had to be the thrones. They were currently unoccupied and the room empty.

"Wait here," he said and veered to the left.

Dane stood there alone in the silence waiting. It gave him time to look around the room. There was no other adornment aside from the flickering torches in brackets along the walls. The only furniture was that of the thrones. Nothing else.

The nobleman returned a moment later and stood beside Dane. The king and his queen entered from a door on the right of the of the room and took their place. The king motioned them closer.

The nobleman gave Dane a nod and stepped forward. He followed him. The man spoke to the king in their native tongue. The king's dark eyes flickered to Dane, question clearly in them. The king replied but Dane had no idea what he said.

"King Ecotzin would like to know where *ta'rin da bara* is," the nobleman said. "He asks you for this information."

Dane peered back at the king. The last time he saw her, he was kissing her against her door. And then he fell ill. Ark

Crane said Ridgewood had plans to take her back to their time. She could be anywhere.

For all he knew, they were already gone. He didn't know what sort of time bender Ridgewood had, or if he had to wait the seventy-two hours as they did. Whatever the case, Dane was having a difficult time suppressing the fear and anxiety coursing through him now. Every minute he delayed was another minute lost.

"I don't know where she is."

"She is not in her suite," the man said. "She has not been seen all day. The king wishes to know why *ta'rin* deserted us in our great time of need."

More alarm trickled through Dane. They'd noticed Skye was missing which meant someone had gone looking for her. Ridgewood got to her first. He must have her.

"Where is the Great One?" Dane demanded.

The king replied without waiting for the man to translate. His words were rapid, urgent.

"What'd he say?"

"He says he needs *ta'rin* here tonight before the full moon rises. Before the Others return. He says *ta'rin* is the only one who can stop them from taking the princess."

Oh, this was getting better and better.

"Who are the Others? Why do they want the princess?"

The king answered as though he understood Dane, but refused to speak the common tongue.

"They come on the full moon and demand a tithe. We have provided what they asked. Now they ask too much," the nobleman translated. "The king believes *ta'rin* can protect the princess and keep them from taking her."

No, *ta'rin* couldn't but perhaps he could. "How long has this been happening? This demand for a tithe?"

"Years," the nobleman said before the king could reply. "Their first requests were simple. Pottery. Arrowheads. But the more they returned, the more they asked for. Animals. Whole crops."

"Why do they want the princess now?" Dane asked.

It was the king who replied, this time in the common tongue. "They want to use my daughter for unspeakable things."

"What kind of things?"

There was a pause. The queen nudged the king. He spoke in his native language.

"Our people are different. Our people have certain abilities, as does the princess. She is special. They want to study her."

Meaning experiments.

Dane clenched his hands into tight fists. "And what do you think *ta'rin* can do to stop them from taking her?"

The king's gaze shifted to the nobleman as he spoke once more in the native tongue. The man translated.

"She is Goddess of Fire, is she not? She has the power of fire, does she not?"

Dane shifted from one foot to the other. This wasn't good. All this time, they both thought they called her that because of her hair color, not because they thought she had some type of magic. Now they were expecting her to do…what exactly? Set them all on fire?

And what was he supposed to tell these people? The Goddess of Fire had no fire magic.

But the more immediate problem was Skye was missing, likely taken by Ridgewood. Until he found her, there was no real reason to tell the king the truth.

"She is, and she does. But you said she hadn't been seen all morning, which tells me she's missing. I believe your Great One has something to do with that."

"Why would he take her away?"

"It's complicated." It was the only answer Dane had. All he knew was Ridgewood planned to take her back home with him. Why, he didn't know. "I have to find her. If we don't find her, then she can't help you. If you expect her to help you before the full moon rises tonight, then I have to find her soon. The day is nearly gone."

The nobleman looked to the king who had a contemplative look on his face. He started to speak, when the queen laid a hand on his arm and leaned closer to him. He turned his head to meet her gaze. She spoke so only he could hear. Her voice was nothing but a murmur. The king stared at her long and hard and then gave one nod of his head before turning back to the two of them.

"Acotl will help you. Take whatever men you need to find her. But find her. Bring her to me here in the Citadel before moonrise. Your king has spoken."

He stood. The queen stood. Together, they left the throne room. It was up to him and Acotl to find Skye.

Dane hoped it wasn't too late.

~ ⧗ ~

Skye followed Tia through the corridors of the Citadel, moving through places she hadn't seen before. She wasn't sure if the girl was taking her through passageways to avoid running into Ridgewood or what.

"Where is this tunnel?" Skye asked.

"It runs under the Citadel and the village."

"I know but where do I go to find it?"

"In a place you know."

Tia turned a corner, Skye on her heels. She recognized the corridor and knew the girl was leading her back to her own suite. Skye grabbed the girl by the arm and spun her around.

"Is this some sort of trick?"

Her eyes were wide and round. "Trick?"

"You're leading me back to my room."

"Yes, it is there."

"What is?"

"The tunnel."

Skye narrowed her eyes unsure she believed the girl. What if the girl was leading her back to Ridgewood? Into a trap? Her grip tightened on the girl's wrist, her fingers digging into her flesh.

"How do I know you're telling the truth?"

"I wish you no harm, *ta'rin*," she whispered. "This I swear."

Skye relaxed her grip and released her. She motioned for her to continue. They hurried down the corridor and entered her room, closing the door behind them. Skye twisted the lock, hoping to keep anyone else out. Tia, meanwhile, made her way across the room into the bathing chamber. Skye followed.

Tia stood at the far end of the room, peering at the tile wall. She pressed on a number of tiles in a strange pattern. A second later, there was a hiss and a passageway opened to darkness.

Skye hesitated as she looked at the escape route. What if she was wrong to go with Tia? What if this was all a mistake and she should go with Ridgewood? He was returning to her time. Even if she was his prisoner, wasn't that better than being trapped in a strange world?

She took a step toward the opening. A demanding knock on her suite door made her halt, her heart in her throat.

"Come. Hurry." Tia was at the opening, pushing the heavy tiled wall open. She slipped inside the darkness.

Another pounding knock. Skye didn't wait for another invitation. She bolted for the opening and stepped inside after Tia. The girl pulled the wall closed, shrouding them in darkness. Skye whimpered, her voice the only sound in the silence. The tunnel was damp and smelled old and musty.

Firelight flickered and exploded in the small space. It took several seconds for Skye to realize it was coming from Tia's hand. The orange and red flames danced her in palm as she used it like a torch. Skye couldn't stop staring.

"Follow me."

The girl took off down the tunnel without looking back.

~ ⧖ ~

The first place Dane started looking for Skye was her room. He didn't think he would find her there, but he had to try. For all he knew, Ridgewood had her locked up in her room.

There were no guards posted outside. Likely there was nothing inside to guard. Or Ridgewood thought it wasn't necessary. He tried the handle. Locked. He knocked. No response. He knocked again. Silence was his response. He jammed his shoulder against the door, trying to shove his way inside. The heavy oak door didn't budge. Acotl put a hand on his shoulder.

"Allow me."

He passed his hand over the lock. A second later it clicked open. He twisted the knob and opened the door.

Dane would be impressed with the noble's hidden talent later. Right now, he had to get to Skye. He rushed inside but found it empty. He checked the terrace and saw nothing. He checked the bathing chamber. He stood there a long moment looking around the room. For a sign of what, he didn't know. He turned to go when something caught his eye.

A gap in the far wall.

He moved closer. He could feel a slight breeze coming through the small half inch opening.

"Does this open?" He pointed to the wall and looked back at Acotl.

"I would not think so."

"There's a gap here," Dane insisted.

He pressed his hand against the wall, trying not to apply a lot of pressure. He didn't want to close it if it was indeed an opening. He needed something to pry it open and glanced around the room. All he saw was a stack of fresh towels.

Acotl joined him at the wall, leaning toward it and giving it a close once-over. He ran his forefinger down the gap and noticed it went from ceiling to floor.

"You may be correct," he said. "It appears to be an opening of some type."

"A secret opening," Dane said.

Acotl ran his hand over the tiles, pausing every so often at certain ones to feel them. "This one is smoother than the others. And so is this one." He met his gaze. "It could lead to a hidden passageway."

"We need to get it open. I think she must have gone through there."

Acotl was nodding before he even finished his sentence. He ran his hand over the tiles again, closing his eyes and feeling them. He hummed a nameless tune, something Dane didn't recognize. A second later, the wall popped open revealing the hidden doorway.

Both men jumped backward and peered into the blackness beyond.

"I…don't believe it," Acotl said.

"We need a torch."

Before he could reply, Dane hurried out of the room, snatched a torch out of one of the brackets in the hallway, and returned a second later. Acotl stood in the opening, leaning into the yawning abyss. When he heard Dane, he stepped back.

"It's a passageway for sure. I can hear distant voices echoing off the walls."

It had to be Skye. Perhaps someone helped her escape. Or maybe it was Ridgewood himself who found the passageway and was trying to sneak away with her. Either way, Dane had to get to her.

Holding the torch aloft, he stepped inside.

Chapter 10
Reunions

In the late afternoon, Ridgewood returned to the dungeon to find Skye's cell empty. He stood staring at the vacant cell, the anger rising in his chest.

If Skye escaped, someone helped her. It wouldn't be the guards. They had no reason to release her and let her get away.

He punished Tia for her failure with lashes across her back but it hadn't made the impact he intended. She must be the one to help Skye escape as payback for his cruelty.

Either that or the man still lived. If he still lived, how could Ark Crane fail to complete such a simple job?

Ridgewood spun from the empty cell. The guards watched him with wide-eyed fear as he stomped back up the steps. He hadn't told anyone he was using the holding cell for his own purposes. If the king found out, it would not sit well with him, though Ridgewood suspected the king would be preoccupied with more important matters. Namely, those they called the Others.

The Others had been his own brilliant invention. Their research and development at Janus had sped along at a brisk pace. So much so they had a major breakthrough. While Ridgewood was busy traveling back and forth between his present and this parallel universe, his scientists and developers were busy making a new improved time travel machine. One that could break through time and dimensions.

While he still had and used the time bender device William Ransom created, he hadn't intended to use it to return to present day with Skye. No, he had intended to use the Others travel ship to return. That ship had brought Ark Crane through time to do a job. A job he couldn't seem to do.

Frustration edged through him as he stalked down the hall toward the servant's quarters, aware he'd lost the trail of the guards. He didn't need them. He needed to find the servant girl anyway, to question her and, if necessary, to punish her again.

When he entered the west wing where the servants resided, he found only a few who lounged in their sparsely decorated rooms. Tia was nowhere to be found.

Annoyed, he headed out of the servant's quarters to return to his own room to formulate a plan. That's when he saw Ark Crank staggering down the hall toward him, his shirt bloodied and his face ashen.

Ridgewood knew then Dane was still alive.

"What the bloody hell are you doing here?" Ridgewood demanded. "And where's the man? You were supposed to kill him."

"He got away." He lifted his hand and showed him the dried blood on it.

"What happened to you, then?"

"He stabbed me. I'm lucky to be alive."

Ridgewood stared at him, wondering if he should kill him now or if he still had some usefulness. "Lucky, indeed. Where is he now?"

"I don't know."

"Did you get the device like I asked?"

Ark visibly swallowed. "No."

He clenched his jaw, the muscles tight with his fury. "The girl is missing. He must be helping her get away. We have to find them before the moonrise. That's when the ship is to return." He moved closer to Ark, dropping his voice. "If you want to be on it, then I suggest you finish your job."

~ ⧖ ~

The tunnel went on forever. Along the way, the darkness gave way to light. Tia no longer had to use her hand to illuminate the corridor. Here, the walls and floor were white marble like that of the Citadel above. The eight-foot ceiling was smooth gray rock. Even though she continued to follow her, Skye started to feel a little claustrophobic.

"When will we be out of here?" she asked.

"Soon," the girl replied. "The tunnel exits in the jungle. From there, we will make our way to the docks."

Tia had it all planned, it seemed. Even though she'd consented to go with her, Skye didn't feel right about it. Not that she had any reason to stay. Dane was dead, after all. Her only way of getting home was lost to her. There was nothing for her here. Now that the thought of never getting home was ever-present, a pang of homesickness hit her hard with a sharp pain in her chest. She would never see her present again and that hurt.

Footfalls behind them made her halt and peer over her shoulder.

"Did you hear that?"

Tia stopped, too, looking behind them. "I heard nothing but our own echoes, *ta'rin.*"

The shuffle of feet on the marble could be heard again. A tingling sensation went through Skye as she stood there, squinting. As if that would make the distance come into focus more. Beyond the edge of light was the shadowed darkness but she could see nothing and no one.

"There's someone following us. Did you close the door?" Fear skittered through her already jangled nerves.

"Yes, *ta'rin.* No one could find us here. Only a few know how to open the secret door. None of them would follow."

The footsteps were getting closer. "Are you certain?"

"I am certain."

Skye wasn't so sure. The longer she looked, the more she thought she saw a form coming out of the shadows with a light bobbing in the space next to it. Her heart thudded hard in her chest. Her breath caught. The tall form emerged into the light carrying a torch. There was someone else. Two men. And one of them had dark hair and piercing green eyes.

"Dane." His name came out on a breathless whisper. "It's him!"

Skye bolted into a run without waiting for Tia. Her legs immediately burned with the sudden exertion as she hurried down the marble corridor, her sandals slapping the floor. He saw her, then, and passed the torch off to his companion as she launched herself at him, throwing her body against his in a violent hug of pure delight. He caught her, his arms wrapping around her as he held her to him.

She had never been so damn happy to see anyone in her life. Skye knew, then, everything was going to be all right.

"He said you were dead."

He gave her a quick squeeze before pulling away. He held her face in his hands, pressed his forehead to hers. "I'm not dead. Not yet."

"Thank God."

"Here's a tip for you. Never assume I'm dead unless you see the body, okay?" He kissed the tip of her nose.

She grinned, her relief palpable. "I'll keep that in mind."

"Good."

He released her as Tia joined them.

"This is Acotl. He helped me find you." Dane motioned the man next to him holding the torch.

He was a tall man with the same coloring as Tia, the same wide, almond-shaped dark eyes and dark wavy hair. His dress was better than hers, marking him as someone a level above a servant.

He gave her a low bow. "It is my honor to assist you, *ta'rin*."

"How did you?" she asked.

"There was a slight gap in the wall in your bathing chamber. Acotl opened it."

Skye glanced at him. "How? Tia said only a few knew how to open the secret passageway."

"I have abilities, as do most of us who are chosen."

Tia had abilities, too. Not only could she heal, but she could make light dance in her hand. Tia was one of the chosen. She wanted to ask more questions, but Dane spoke before she could get them out.

"Skye, there's not much time. We have to get back to the Citadel."

She was shaking her head before he finished. "I'm not going back there. Ridgewood tried to take me back with him."

"I know, but there's something more important we have to do. I made a promise to the king."

She stared at him as her mouth went dry. "Why do I have a bad feeling about that?"

"I'll explain on the way." He looked at Tia. "Is there another way out of here?"

"Only one way out." She pointed behind her. "The tunnel exits in the jungle."

"Then we go that way." He took Skye by the hand and gave a nod to Tia. "Lead the way."

Chapter 11
Attack!

Tia led them through the tunnel toward the exit. While they walked, Dane relayed the story to her about his run-in with Ark Crane and how he got away. Skye told him about Ridgewood locking her in the dungeon with the intent of taking her back with him. All the while, Dane eyed the lashes on the girl's back.

"What happened to her?" He kept his voice low.

"Ridgewood punished her."

She could see a muscle tick under his left eye as he stared at those lashes on her back. His mind was at work, perhaps trying to come up with a horrible way to torture the man.

"What I don't understand is what he wants with me." It was a rhetorical statement, she knew. She didn't expect Dane to have an answer.

"Whatever it is, he's determined. He intended to separate us from the start. He nearly succeeded."

"And have you killed," she added. She squeezed his hand grateful he was still alive. "He nearly succeeded at that, too. Do you still have it?"

"Yes." He knew she meant the time bender.

She blew out a breath of relief.

"But I'm not sure how much time we have left," he said. "I haven't had a chance to look at it."

"What happens if time has run out?" She cut him a glance.

He shrugged. "I don't know. We'll have to wait and see after we help the king."

Which reminded her… "What is this thing you promised the king?"

"The king says the Others will come at moonrise to take his daughter." He told her about the tithe the Others asked for with each subsequent visit and that, finally, they wanted the princess.

She had a sneaking suspicion she knew the promise he'd made to the king. At the moment, she was more preoccupied with something else.

"The Others have to be what we saw last night over the Citadel," Skye said. "But who are they?"

"Hard to say. Whoever they are, it's clear they have advanced technologies."

Skye was aware he hadn't told her everything and it made her nervous. "Are you going to tell me about this promise?"

Dane's gaze flickered from Acotl back to her. "He wants you to help protect his daughter."

"How?" She didn't like the sound of this.

"He thinks you have magic because you are the Goddess of Fire."

Nope, she didn't like the sound of this at all. "And what did you tell him?"

"Uh…"

"I don't have magic, Dane."

"I know."

"What did you promise him?" Her heart did a weird thud and suddenly she felt like she was going to throw up.

"Nothing, exactly, but I think he's expecting something spectacular."

She didn't like the sound of that. Hot pinpricks went over her skin.

They came to the end of the tunnel. There didn't appear to be a door. Tia halted. Her hands roamed over the wall, her fingers pausing every so often in certain places. A pop and a hiss and a door opened. Late afternoon sunlight spilled through the opening.

"The tunnel exit."

"We'll figure something out." Dane squeezed her hand as they exited into the jungle.

The oppressive humidity immediately smacked her in the face. In the not-so-far distance, Skye could swear she heard the lapping of waves and men's voices calling out.

Once they were out, Tia turned back to the opening, did her thing with her hands and closed the tunnel. It sealed up again, and a moment later, appeared as though it was part of the rocks. Lifting her eyes, Skye could see they were standing outside a rocky outcropping. Beyond that, she could see the top of the Citadel.

"We're a long way from the palace," she said.

Dane followed her gaze realizing the distance between them and the Citadel. He released Skye's hand and whirled on Tia.

"How far are we from the Citadel?"

Her gaze flickered from his angry face upward to the palace sitting atop the hill behind them.

"*How far?*" His voice was hard and cold.

"Dane, leave her be." Skye put a hand on his arm. "She got us out of the tunnel."

"Your pardon," Acotl said, "but the sun slips toward the horizon. It won't be long before moonrise and then the Others return."

Tia backed away from them, eyes wide as she shook her head. "I am not returning."

Skye knew why. She took a tentative step toward her, but she backed up again. "Tia, I promised you Ridgewood wouldn't hurt you again, didn't I? I promised we would protect you." She motioned between her and Dane.

The girl's gaze flickered between them. She gave a slow nod.

"And I meant it. But we have to go back and help the princess." Skye took another step toward her, reached for her hand and took it. "You have a precious gift. You can help us."

"I can?" Her voice was a whisper.

Skye nodded as she lifted the girl's hand up, palm open. "You can. Remember what you did in the tunnel?"

Her reply was the spark of light in her open hand. How she managed to do that, Skye would never know.

"You can make fire in your hand?" Dane moved to stand next to Skye, peering at the flames flickering in the girl's palm.

Tia nodded.

"She can." Skye met Dane's gaze. "I have an idea."

He grinned. "Brilliant girl. How long will it take us to get back to the Citadel?"

"Hours," Acotl said. "The docks are just there." He pointed through the trees. "The merchant ships will be leaving at dusk."

Tia let out a small whimper. The ship she was, no doubt, supposed to be on. Skye reached for her and patted her shoulder in reassurance. She would find a way to get that girl on another ship if it was the last thing she did.

"Tia, will there be another ship tomorrow?"

The girl bit her lower lip and nodded. "In the morning."

"I swear to you we will get you on that ship tomorrow." She paused, formulating her next words carefully. "If you could do something for me."

"For you, *ta'rin da bara*?"

Skye nodded. "Yes, for me. A favor."

"What is favor?"

"A…boon. A kindness. A special task," Skye explained. "Do you think you could do that for me?"

Skye could tell the girl was considering. She at last gave a nod. "Yes, *ta'rin*."

"Nice work," Dane said quietly. "What's the plan?"

~ ⧗ ~

Sweat dampened Skye's entire body as they trekked through the jungle making their way back to the Citadel. As the sun dipped lower and lower to the horizon, she knew they were running out of time. Her heart was in her throat the whole time.

None of them spoke much. The closer they got to the Citadel the sadder Tia looked. Skye knew the girl was doing this for her. Their plan wasn't foolproof, but perhaps would be enough to save the princess. They would have to figure out what to do about Ridgewood once the princess was safe.

Dusk stained the sky a pale indigo and pink as the sun set. As they neared the Citadel, they could hear pounding drums in a *ba-da-boom-ba-da-boom*. Tia gasped and pressed her fingers against her lips.

"What is it?" Dane asked her.

She didn't respond. She moved through the foliage and pushed it aside, giving them an unobstructed view. The princess walked down the steps of the Citadel flanked by two men. Ridgewood followed a few steps behind them. The king and queen stood at the top of the stone steps watching the princess descend.

"What does it mean?" Skye wanted to know.

"She goes to meet her fate. We are too late." Acotl expression was grim.

Dane swore under his breath. Skye could see his pulse throbbing in his neck. "We need a distraction."

"What do you suggest?" Skye asked.

"Anything."

"If you will permit me?" Acotl said.

Dane gave him a nod.

"Wait here."

He took off through the jungle, disappearing through the foliage at the edge of the village.

"Great. Now what?" Skye huffed out a breath.

"We wait, like he said," Dane replied.

She heaved a sigh and found a fallen log to sit on. She had never been so sweaty, thirsty, and tired. Long, hot minutes ticked by. Minutes she couldn't count because she'd long since lost her watch or any way to tell time. She didn't even have a smartphone anymore.

She gave Dane a sideways glance as he crouched in the jungle, peering through the leaves and watching for Acotl's return. Dane was her only salvation. Her only sense of belonging. If she lost him, she wasn't sure how she'd cope. And she'd come close to losing him. When she thought Ridgewood had killed him, she had never felt so isolated or alone before in her life. Even after the death of her parents, she still had friends and other extended family she could lean on. But here, lost in time, Dane was the only one she had. She had a profound sense of relief when she found him alive and well.

"What?" His voice shattered the tense silence, cutting through the humidity.

Her eyes flew open wide. Had she been staring at him and not realized it? And how did he know she was staring?

"I didn't say anything," she said.

"You keep looking at me. What is it, Skye?"

Did the man have eyes in the back of his head? How did he know that? She inhaled a deep breath through her nose. She had no intention of revealing her thoughts. "Nothing."

He turned his head to look at her, his glittering green gaze meeting hers. "Don't 'nothing' me. There's something."

She huffed out a breath. "It's just that…well, I'm glad you're not dead."

Something softened in his gaze. Tension released from his shoulders. "Me, too."

He turned back to peer through the jungle leaves again, keeping a watchful eye on the village beyond. She ran her fingers through her sweat-dampened hair, ready to give up waiting on the man when there was a sudden high-pitched cry coming from the village. She jumped to her feet.

"Oh, shit," Dane muttered.

"What the hell is that?" she asked.

"The war cry," Tia said.

"What does that mean?" Skye asked.

"It means they are attacking the Citadel."

"That's his idea of a distraction?" Dane shook his head and huffed out a breath. "What are we supposed to do now?"

Skye gave him a shrug. "Join the fray?"

He stared at her a long moment trying to decide if that was the best course of action. She could see his mind working behind those sharp eyes of his and she knew he was working it out, thinking of all the scenarios and anything that could go wrong.

"We can't hide in the jungle, Dane," she urged.

"I hope you know what you're doing."

Dane stepped out of the jungle. Skye followed with Tia behind her. They halted, though, as soon as they saw the scene. Men held their spears and ran through the village toward the Citadel, heading right for the princess and Ridgewood. They would intercept them before long.

The two men escorting the princess unsheathed their weapons—each held a long spear and crossed it in front of the princess in an X formation. As though that would stop the men from coming. It didn't. They barreled right for them, yelling their war cry. Behind them, the king took action. He made a hand signal to someone they couldn't see standing nearby. Guards poured out of the Citadel and rushed down the steps of the Citadel bellowing their own war cries.

Ridgewood halted, his head swiveling back and forth as though trying to decide what to do next. He was faced with the village men heading toward him. Behind him, Citadel guards swarmed to take on the attackers. In an odd move, he lifted his fisted hand to his mouth. It looked like he said something into his wrist.

"Dane, did you see that?" She looked at him and saw his gaze was pinned on Ridgewood.

"I did. He has a communication device."

"Who is he communicating with?"

He flashed her a smile. "I'll find out. You two stay put."

"But—"

"I mean it, Skye. Let me handle this."

She knew he was right, but she didn't have to like it. She gave him a reluctant nod. He started to head toward Ridgewood, halted, turned back to her. Before she had time to react, he kissed her quick, hard, and fast. She barely got a taste of him before he pulled away and was off again. He didn't blend in with the natives. His sun-kissed skin was still a few shades lighter than theirs. But he ran with them heading right toward the princess, the two guards, and Ridgewood.

The guards and villagers collided, their war cries and clashing weapons a cacophony of noise. Skye tensed when she realized Dane made a zigzag through the men, heading directly for Ridgewood. He saw him, too. Even from her distance, she could see surprise, then anger flicker over his face. He lifted his wrist again and spoke, his mouth moved with what she could guess was urgency. Whoever was on the other end of that communication, he wanted to get their attention in a hurry.

Tia nudged her and pointed to the east, saying nothing. It was full on sunset now and the moon had started a slow ascent in the deepening twilight. As Skye watched, she marveled at the quick pace the moon rose, full and bright.

"The Others are coming," Tia said, then.

"How do you know?"

She didn't answer, only pointed upward again.

Skye saw it then. The thing that had descended upon the Citadel the night of the feast arrived. That was the night they had given her offerings in the hopes she would save them. From her vantage point, she could make out the outline of it and saw it looked oddly like a ship. A spaceship? A plane? Definitely some kind of flying machine. It was hard to make out in the cascading darkness, but she could see an outline of it and a few twinkling lights that tended to blend in with the stars above, camouflaging it.

The machine hovered over the top of the Citadel, catching the attention of the king and queen. Both tipped their heads back to look up at the thing. The sudden appearance of the machine wreaked havoc on the guards and villagers alike, making them stop the fighting.

Skye's gaze flew to Dane in time to see one of the guards throw a punch, catching him in the jaw. Dane collapsed to the ground, but appeared to otherwise be all right. The guard noticed the arrival of the machine and forgot Dane existed as he turned his attention to it.

Ridgewood made a hand signal to someone above in the machine, as though telling the pilot where to land. Then he dove for the princess, wrapped his arms around her waist and dragged her away from the guards who were trying to protect her. The girl kicked and screamed, protesting with every step Ridgewood took back toward the Citadel, toward the stone steps.

Skye knew she and Tia had to act quickly. They had to get to the princess before that ship landed and before Ridgewood dragged her onto it.

She clamped a hand around Tia's wrist. "Come on. We have to stop them."

But before she could take a step, a sharp tip pierced her lower back followed by a harsh, deep voice she knew. "Move and you die."

Ark Crane found her.

Chapter 12
Goddess of Fire

Dane didn't account for how quick the guard's reflexes were. When he landed a punch, he didn't expect for it to knock him off his feet. He tumbled to the ground. As he flipped over, ready to jump to his feet, he saw what had caught the attention of the men and why they stopped fighting.

He could see the machine over the Citadel, could make out an outline of the thing. He couldn't tell exactly what it was in the darkness.

Then he caught sight of Ridgewood dragging the princess away. He swore under his breath and started for him. Behind him, a sharp female cry made him halt and spin around. Ark Crane had Skye by the hair, dragging her down the village road. When Tia protested, he backhanded her hard. The girl crashed to the ground in a heap, dirt flying up around her.

Dane clenched his fists and took off at a dead run toward Ark and Skye.

Gunshots rang out behind him. He skidded to a halt and spun back around to see Ridgewood holding a hand gun, pointing it toward the men who tried to stop him from taking the princess. He shot and killed one of them. Torn, he glanced back at Skye. Ark placed a knife at her throat. She clutched his meaty forearm as he pulled her along, stumbling and backing down the road.

Another gunshot and another villager went down. This time it was Acotl. Dane bolted toward the man, dropping to his knees when he got to him. Blood spread on the nobleman's tunic from the bullet lodged in his chest. He'd died instantly. Dane brushed his hand over his face, closing his eyes for the last time.

Fury welled inside him as he looked up at Ridgewood who now pointed the gun toward him. Warning was written all over his face as he dragged the princess away and started back up the stone steps. Only when he heard the panting next to him did he realize Tia was by his side. Sweat dripped down the side of her face and dust covered her sandaled feet. Her lip was swollen and bloody where Ark hit her. She gulped in great gasps of air into her lungs, trying to catch her breath. She nudged Dane aside and reached for Acotl, placing her hands over his bloodied shirt.

"He's gone," Dane said. "You can't save him. I'm sorry."

She lifted her gaze to his, tears welling in her eyes. She shook it off and gripped his arm, her fingers digging into flesh.

"He's…taking…her…" She pointed back to Skye and Ark.

Dane saw. He knew. But Ark had turned off the main road and headed through the jungle.

"Where?" he demanded.

She shook her head. "I…don't know."

He had to follow her, but he had to do something about the princess, too. He looked back at the machine which started to lower toward the ground on the backside of the Citadel.

In the courtyard area.

That's where Ridgewood was going. That must be where Ark was taking Skye. Ridgewood had said he wanted to take her back to their time with him. Why, then, did he want the princess? Something didn't make sense.

"What's the fastest way to the courtyard?" Dane asked the girl.

She sucked in a deep breath of air, finally calming her heaving chest. "There is only one way. Through the Citadel."

"There has to be another way," Dane insisted. He glanced back to where Ark disappeared through the trees with Skye. If he wasn't going to the courtyard, then where? He gripped the girl by the upper arms. "They're taking both women to the courtyard. I have to get there *now*."

She swallowed hard, shaking her head. "There is no other—"

"There is," a man broke in. He stepped forward. His dress was similar to that of Acotl, so Dane assumed he was another nobleman. "If I show you, you will help the princess and *ta'rin da bara*?"

"I will," Dane said.

"Then follow me." He motioned for him to follow and took off at a run.

Dane glanced back at Tia and, in a split-second decision, he grabbed her by the hand and started to run.

~ ⧗ ~

The large bloodstain on Ark's tunic didn't escape Skye's notice. Nor did the foul stench emanating off him, as if he hadn't bathed in days. She also noted the man limped and grunted. She knew he was injured and trying to do his job still. Sweat bathed his face and neck.

When he wrapped his meaty arm around her, the knife point at her throat, she had no choice but to go with him. Even though it had angered her when he smacked Tia. She could do nothing to stop him from hitting the girl, just as Tia couldn't stop him from taking her away from the village.

They left the main road and headed back into the jungle. The last thing she saw was Dane standing in the middle of the village road watching Ridgewood steal the princess. Was that a gun Ridgewood held? When the gunshots went off, she was certain he had somehow armed himself. He'd brought weapons from their time, their dimension, not caring about altering this world by bringing weapons here.

Her only hope was Tia had the sense to get to Dane and follow through with their plan. The only way the villagers were going to see she was not this Goddess of Fire was if Tia was brave enough to do what she needed her to do. Tia had the gift of fire magic. She was the true *ta'rin da bara*. She was the one who could save them all from Ridgewood and the Others. Not her.

"Why don't you let me go?" Skye said.

"Shut up," he snarled in her ear.

"It's obvious you're injured. You need a healer or a doctor or something."

"I said, shut up, you stupid bitch." He pressed the knife closer to her skin, nicking her.

She clenched her jaw but remained silent as he dragged her through the jungle. They had doubled back and headed once again for the Citadel. He was taking her back, likely to Ridgewood. She had no way out of this. All she could do was follow along, at the hit man's mercy.

They stumbled out of the jungle to a stone wall that rose up high overhead. Glancing upward, she could see it was part of the Citadel. He removed the knife and clamped his hand on her wrist, dragging her down the length of the wall. She stumbled along after him. With his free hand, he clutched his side and groaned in pain.

"Where are we going?" she asked.

He didn't answer as he came to a wooden door with iron hinges. It looked old and odd in the middle of the stone wall. How had he found this place? He shoved open the door, then gave her wrist a jerk and pushed her through. He followed, closing it behind them.

By now, the moon was high in the sky and she could see they were in a garden bathed in the soft light. He grabbed her wrist again. But as he took a step, the pain must have overcome him because he crumpled and fell to his hands and knees. She could see his tunic glistened with fresh blood.

"You need a healer," she said.

She kneeled next to him and looked him over. His face was pinched with pain, his jaw clenched and tight.

"Your bodyguard tried to kill me but didn't succeed." He pulled up the bloodstained shirt and showed her the crude bandage soaked in red. "A healer tried but the stitches aren't holding."

Dane had stabbed him? He must have done it to get away from him.

Ark started to laugh then, as though he'd thought of something hilarious. "I'm supposed to bring you to Ridgewood." He laid back in the grass, staring up at the night sky.

"But?" It sounded as if he had more to say.

"He's planning to kill me anyway. I should just die here." He laughed again, a bitter sound.

Skye started at him, unsure what she should do. She bit her lip.

"I murdered your parents," he said then.

The unexpectedness of his words sent a pang though her. Her heart stuttered and hot tears sprang to her eyes and clotted her throat.

"Who hired you?" she managed.

"Does it matter?" His head lolled from side to side as he pressed his hand against his side. Blood seeped through his fingers.

"Yes, to me it does."

"Connor Dade, that bastard."

She knew it. He'd come snooping around the house after the funerals acting odd. She suspected then, but it didn't explain Ridgewood.

"Is he working for Ridgewood?"

He chuckled. "He is now. We both are."

"Who is he?"

"Damn, girl, you have a lot of questions. Now, go away and let me die in peace."

His eyes fluttered closed as she stared down at him. He was letting her go? Just like that?

"The courtyard is a hundred yards away."

Skye sat, immobile, looking down at him. Her mind had ceased to function.

"Get out of here," he barked.

She shoved upward to her feet, gave him one last glance, and took off at a dead run.

~ ⧖ ~

Dane dragged poor Tia along as he followed the man around the side of the building. The Citadel sat on top of a hill, so their trek was straight up. His legs burned with the fierce fire of exertion. Even though he was in shape, the rushed climb left him gasping for air. He could hear Tia's breath wheezing in and out as she struggled to keep up.

Guilt swarmed through him, but he couldn't let her go. He needed her.

As they followed the wall around the Citadel, they came to a break in it, as though it had a weak spot and crumbled from age. The man led them through it, carefully picking his way over the rocks and debris. Dane helped Tia across and then hurried after the nobleman. They were in the courtyard now, in a part of it he hadn't seen before. Above them, the machine hovered, waiting.

They were on a cracked path now. Weeds and grass had overgrown the pave stones that led through the garden. He pushed aside large leaves of a tree and motioned for the two of them to go through. Dane halted next to the man.

"This is where I leave you," he said.

Dane understood. He didn't want any part of what was to come. "Thank you."

"I wish you good fortune." His gaze flickered to Tia, who tried hard to catch her breath. "And to you, healer."

She bowed her head in acknowledgement but said nothing. Still holding her by the wrist, Dane led her through the foliage. As he stepped into the clearing, he took in the empty courtyard. Gone was the long table and chairs, the dais and the chair Skye had sat upon during the feast. The only thing left was the monolith which remained unlit.

On the other side, someone came crashing through the leaves. Her fiery hair was unmistakable in the moonlight. She tripped and collided with the ground. At first, he thought Ark had pushed her, but the hit man didn't make an appearance. She was alone.

At the sight of her, Tia gasped, then whispered, *"Ta'rin."*

Skye picked herself up off the ground. She had grass stains on her clothes and dirt on her knees.

As she moved deep into the courtyard, he and Tia made their way toward her. She caught sight of him and her face broke into a wide smile. She darted toward him, her hair flying behind her. A gunshot rang out. She dropped to the ground with a cry.

Ridgewood stood on the other side of the courtyard, near the Citadel entrance, the gun in his hand. He turned the gun on the princess, pressing it against her head.

"Take another step and she dies."

Dane released Tia's hand and held up his in surrender. "All right. You win."

Still holding the princess, he walked toward Skye who climbed to her feet. Blood smeared down her arm. Her defiant gaze met Ridgewood's.

"You missed," she said.

He smirked. "Did I? You're bleeding."

"Let the princess go, Ridgewood," Dane called.

He halted, removed the gun from the princess's head and pointed it at Skye. "I cannot. I'm afraid she has to come with me, too."

"Why?"

"Because her people have a unique genetic strand we want to study." Ridgewood had a slimy smirk on his face as though he was excited about the thought of dissecting the princess.

"Who's 'we'?" Skye asked.

"You'll know soon enough." He waved her in front of him with the gun. "Let's go."

Overhead, the machine lowered closer to the ground. The courtyard was big enough to allow the thing to land. It wasn't as large as Dane first thought. It looked like nothing more than a small shuttle, reminding him a little of something out of Star Trek. A door slid open, but no one appeared inside.

"Get in," Ridgewood said.

Skye looked at him, then, her gaze pleading. He had to stop this. He had to keep her from getting on that ship. He looked around for anything he could use as a weapon but found nothing.

Tia stepped around him, putting herself between him and Ridgewood. Her hands glowed bright white.

"Stop." Her voice rang out across the courtyard.

Skye's eyes widened at the girl. Dane's head snapped to her.

"Tia, what are you doing?" he said, voice low.

Ridgewood laughed at her. "Or what?"

Tia walked to stand in front of him. Skye glanced at him, then back at Tia's glowing hands. Dane took slow steps toward them, keeping an eye on Ridgewood waiting for an opportunity. His gun hand went slack as he pinned the girl with his bright blue gaze.

"What are you planning to do, girl? Kill me?" He shook his head. "You can't touch me."

The white glow turned orange and red and yellow, flickering like a flame.

"Tia?" Skye queried.

Dane couldn't get close to any of them. Tia stood in between him and Ridgewood, the princess and Skye. He waved his gun between the women, as if trying to decide who to shoot first.

"Ridgewood, let the princess go. She doesn't belong where you're going," Dane said. "You know that as well as I do."

He pointed the gun at Dane. "If I wanted your opinion, I would have asked for it."

At the entrance to the Citadel, the king appeared flanked by several guards. He spotted his daughter. She cried out to him in her native tongue. Enraged, Ridgewood shoved the princess toward the ship. She stumbled forward, bashed her shins on the ledge and fell inside. He turned to Skye next.

"Get. In." His words were sharp and stilted.

Skye cut Dane a glance and their eyes met. She mouthed the word *sorry*. His gut twisted as he watched her make the final decision, the only one she could. Blood stained the shoulder of her tunic dress.

She held her hands up and stepped toward the ship. The princess huddled on the floor, crying and speaking in her own tongue, the words sounding like a prayer.

Tia looked at him, then, her eyes blazing fury. "There is only one way to save them."

Dane knew what she meant. He gave her a nod. "Do what you have to."

The girl shrieked her own war cry as she lunched her small body toward Ridgewood, her flaming hands outstretched toward him. His eyes flew wide as he watched the raging girl barrel toward him. Dane took off at a run and skirted around her. He got to Skye and the princess as Ridgewood fell into the side of the ship to avoid Tia's flaming hands. But she didn't go for him. She went for the gun. Her hands clamped around the barrel, turning it from black to as red as a hot poker. Ridgewood shrieked and dropped the weapon, holding his wrist as smoke drifted off his skin. The stench of burned flesh filled the air.

Skye gathered the princess, pulling her close as Dane reached them. Relief flooded her face as he wrapped a protective arm around her and they stumbled away from the ship.

Behind them, Tia shot flames from her hands, narrowly missing Ridgewood. He cried out as he staggered toward the opening in the ship. He toppled inside just as Tia sent another bolt of light from her hands, charring the outside of it. The door slid shut and the machine lifted toward the sky.

But Tia wasn't done yet. In her anger and rage, she lifted her hands toward the sky, screamed that war cry as fire exploded from her fingertips. The flames licked the bottom of the machine as it made its way into the night sky. A quick flash of light and then the thing disappeared and was gone.

Next to him, a breath shuddered out of Skye. "He's gone."

He was gone, but he would be back.

Chapter 13
Aftermath

As soon as the machine winked out of existence, Tia collapsed to the ground. Skye didn't bother to stifle her gasp as she wiggled out of Dane's protective arm and ran to the girl. She dropped to her knees beside her, rolling her to her back and calling her name. The girl was out cold.

Dane knelt next to Skye. He pressed two fingers against the girl's throat to check for a pulse.

"She's alive," he said. "Maybe whatever she did drained her?"

The king and princess moved to stand across from them, looking down at the unconscious Tia. They conversed in their native tongue. The only words Skye recognized was *ta'rin da bara,* which caught her attention. She looked up at the king and his daughter, meeting the princess's eyes.

"She is the one." Skye motioned to Tia. She didn't know if the princess understood her but she hoped with her hand motions she would get it.

"Goddess of Fire," the princess said, her words stilted English.

Surprise flickered through her that she could speak the common tongue. "Yes," Skye said with a nod.

The king spoke, his words frenetic. The princess nodded to whatever he said and then left them, returning to the Citadel. The king remained, though, standing like a sentry over them.

"What do we do now?" Skye kept her voice low so only Dane could hear. She was uncomfortable under the scrutiny of the king.

Dane's sharp green gaze was on the entrance to the Citadel. He kept it there when he replied. "I don't know."

"Do you think she's all right?"

"Yes," Dane said, still not looking at her.

"I honestly didn't think what she did would be that spectacular. I knew she had fire, but I didn't know she had that much fire."

Skye knew he wasn't really listening and that was okay by her. She rambled anyway. She brushed a lock of hair off the girl's forehead. She noticed the painted markings still on her arms and hands faded to almost nothing. The paint had flecked off during all the excitement. Those were the markings Tia placed on her insisting she was the Goddess of Fire.

Who knew it was actually Tia?

Well, she wasn't sure if Tia *was* the goddess, but whatever magic she possessed certainly indicated she could be. When Skye suggested she help them in that way, she had no idea the girl was so powerful. Perhaps even Tia had no idea she was so powerful until her anger fueled her.

The princess exited into the courtyard, leading several men with her. They carried between them a crude stretcher made from two long poles and thick material stretched between them. Skye and Dane got to their feet and moved out of the way. The men lifted the unconscious girl onto the stretcher and then took her away, back into the Citadel.

The princess watched them take her away, then turned her gaze to the two of them. Skye inched a little closer to Dane as the princess approached them.

"You have brought us a great gift." She bowed her head toward Skye in thanks. "She saved us from the Others and the Great One."

"Not such a Great One," Skye muttered.

"Will she be all right?" Dane asked.

The princess gave him a nod. "She will live. She needs rest, though. The fire magic burned through her."

"Why did he want you?" Dane asked.

"Because I am royalty and this." She lifted her hand. Snowflakes danced along her fingertips.

So, the princess had her own magic and Ridgewood knew it.

"He told me I was special and I needed to come with him to a place that would honor me. But I did not wish to go. I knew he would never allow me to stay here. I thank you both for your help." She paused and looked back at Tia. "When she wakes, she will be honored with a feast. We will give her whatever her heart desires."

Skye cleared her throat. "I believe the only thing her heart desires is to go home."

"Home?" The princess wrinkled her brow in question and tipped her head to the side, as if the very idea the Citadel wasn't her home was foreign to her. "Is this not her home?"

"No," Skye said. "Tia told me she was stolen away from her mother when she was a child and brought here."

The king spoke to his daughter who nodded. She turned back to the two of them. "Then if that is what she truly wants, we will see to it she's set free and returns. In the meantime, come. Rest." She waved toward the Citadel.

As soon as the words were out of her mouth, exhaustion pounded through Skye. Her legs were leaden. She was tired and hungry and really wanted a bath. The princess led them through the Citadel to a different wing. This was not the same rooms as before when Ridgewood led them through the palace. They walked in silence behind the princess and she thought of everything that had happened in this strange place.

The princess stopped at a door and motioned to it. "Your room. You'll find everything you need for your comforts."

"Only one room?" Dane asked.

Skye thought she sensed a bit of alarm behind his words but his face remained impassive.

"Yes, only one. Are you not mates? You travel together, yes?"

Skye coughed loudly to cover the laugh that wanted to erupt. Dane gave her a sideways glance of aggravation.

"One room will be fine," he said.

She bowed and left. Skye stared after her suddenly aware of the loud throb of her heart in her ears. They were supposed to share the room? She thought they were mates because they traveled together? She swallowed hard.

Dane seemed unfazed by the idea despite questioning it. He reached for the knob, twisted it, and shoved open the door. She followed him inside as he gave out a low whistle.

Her other room was palatial but this one…this one was like her small apartment back home except fancier. The ceiling soared at least twenty feet with an intricate wood-carved design with the accents painted gold. A small seating area hosted several low-backed plush chairs, a plush rug, a low dark brown wood table. A bowl of fresh fruit rested on top of it. Next to the bowl, a clear pitcher with water and two goblets.

There was a room off to the left that was the bathing chamber much like the one in her previous room. To the right, the bedroom. The only bedroom. With one bed. Her heart pounded as she peered into the room with the silk-draped four-posted bed piled high with pillows and covered with a silk coverlet.

Behind the sitting area, terrace doors with a view of the other side of the Citadel. Through the panes of glass, they could see nothing but the night. Dane moved to the doors and opened them, allowing the cool night air to spill inside.

He disappeared into the shadows. "Skye, come see."

She followed him outside. As soon as she stepped onto the terrace, she smelled the sweet scent of flowers. She joined him at the railing. The view stole her breath. Below them was the palace gardens with pathways bathed in a soft light from strategically placed gas lamps. Greenery, flowers, a hedge maze. It was a feast for her eyes and she only wished the sun was out so she could take in all the colors of the garden.

"Maybe in the morning, we can see more detail," he said.

"Maybe." She nodded.

He turned to her then and when he looked at her, something shifted through her. Her heart sped up. A cold sweat broke out on her palms. "I guess we're sharing."

She nodded, biting her lip. They'd shared two kisses and had yet to discuss either of them. It hung between them like a family secret neither of them were willing to discuss. He started to say something, then stopped and faced the shadowed garden again.

"You know it's not over with Ridgewood, right?" His voice was thick with something that sounded like worry.

"I know. Somehow, he's figured out how to make a time travel machine much bigger than the one we have," she said. "I don't know how he did it unless my father had something like it in his designs. And we don't even know *who* Ridgewood is."

"No," he agreed. "But he's after you and he wants me dead. That much is certain."

He reached into his pocket and brought out the small device. He held it in his palm. They both looked down at it. The date had finally reset. Seeing it made her heart sink and she didn't even know why.

"Looks like we can time jump now," he said.

She reached for his hand, closed his fingers around the device. "Not yet."

"You want to make sure Tia is all right, don't you?"

She lifted her eyes, met his gaze. "I promised I would see her to that ship. That *we* would see her to that ship. I want to keep that promise. If that's all right with you?"

Compassion and understanding flickered in his eyes as a small smile lifted one corner of his mouth. "It is." He pocketed the device. "There's something I want to ask you."

She swallowed hard, her nerves on edge. "Okay."

"What happened to Ark Crane?"

She shrugged. "He let me go."

His jaw hardened. "He's still out there then?"

"Somewhere. I doubt he's going to live much longer. He was wounded and bleeding pretty badly. You stabbed him, didn't you?"

"I had to get to you." He said it matter-of-fact, unapologetic. Like stabbing a man to get back to her was nothing.

It made her heart stumble. She would never forget the way his face looked when she tumbled out of the foliage of the courtyard and saw him on the other side. Relief then joy flickered over his features. She didn't know how he made it to the Citadel and it didn't matter. All that mattered was he'd found her again.

"I made a promise, too," he said then, his voice low.

Her stomach clenched with heated desire. She didn't want to be attracted to Dane, but she couldn't stop those feelings of need and want pouring through her. When she thought he was dead, she had almost lost all hope at the thought of being trapped in time. But he'd made his way back to her because he had promised her father he'd keep her safe. A promise he was clearly determined to keep no matter what.

He turned back to the gardens, his hands on the handrail gripping it tight. His nail beds leached of color. She noticed. "You should clean up and get some sleep."

"What about you?"

What was she saying? She couldn't control her mouth and wasn't sure what she meant. Did she want him to bathe with her? Sleep next to her in that bed with all the silk draperies and pillows and coverlet? She tried *not* to think about how their slick, naked bodies would feel against those slick, satin sheets but the more she tried not to think about it, the more she thought about it. She hated herself.

"I'll be here for a while." He glanced at her, gave her a smile and jerked his head toward the door. "Go ahead."

She stepped inside and made her way to the bathing chamber. They still hadn't talked about the kiss. She wasn't even sure why she needed to talk about it. He seemed perfectly content to kiss her and nothing more. But she couldn't help but wonder what it meant and why she liked it so much.

~ ⧗ ~

Dane listened to her receding footsteps as he stood on the terrace. Below, night creatures sang softly but all he could think about was Skye and the way her face softened when he told her he made a promise, too. Or the way relief flooded her pretty face when she saw him in the tunnel. Or the way her mouth felt when he kissed her. Or the way her body shuddered when he held her.

Hells bells.

He wasn't sure how much longer he could keep that promise to keep her alive. Every time they made a time jump was another instance putting her life—and his—in danger. With every landing, every leap into a new world, things between them shifted and changed.

Kissing her was the worst idea ever, no matter how much he liked it.

He dug the tips of his fingers into the railing breaking off what little nails he had left. Standing in the cool night air was the only thing keeping the heat of desire at bay. He resisted marching inside and taking her to that sumptuous bed covered in silk and satin. In the short time they knew each other, she'd gotten under his skin.

He had to remind himself she was young. She was far too young for him. She wasn't his type. She was nothing like the women he'd dated in the past. She was smart, but naïve. She was resourceful, but inexperienced. She was sweet and beautiful and compassionate and kind.

She was everything.

And her hair. God, that thick wavy copper hair. He wanted to drag his fingers through it.

"Dane?"

Her voice behind him made him jump. How long had he been standing there brooding?

He turned to face her and his heart nearly stopped. She wore a clean knee-length tunic dress in a soft butter yellow that clung to her youthful, curvy body. Her legs and feet were bare. Her hair was damp and pulled over one shoulder, the tips stopping just above the swell of her breast. Her skin was scrubbed clean of all the markings he'd jokingly called war paint. Her upturned face was lit by the soft candlelight of the room behind her as she paused inside the doorway looking at him with those inquisitive indigo eyes. Whatever she saw in his expression made her breath shudder out of her.

He wanted to tell her not to do that, but he couldn't. Words froze in his throat as he looked at her and all he knew was he wanted her.

"I'm done in the bathroom."

She stifled a yawn as she back away from the door, turned on her heel and hurried away from the terrace. Her bare feet padded into the bedroom. He heard her breath as she blew out the candles and then the whisper of material as she slipped under that satin coverlet.

Dane turned back to the view of the gardens and knew he'd be sleeping out there tonight.

Chapter 14
In the Dawning

Skye curled on her side, her eyes wide open to the shadowed darkness. Her body vibrated, her tensions stretched thin. She listened for signs of movement in the rest of the room. There was only silence. Not even the scrape of a chair or the swish of the door closing.

Dane wasn't coming.

It was just as well. She wasn't sure how she felt about being in the same room with him. He hadn't given her any indication he was interested romantically in her since that last kiss. Sure, he'd found her in the tunnel. Sure, he'd told her he had a promise to keep—one to her dead father to keep her safe and out of the hands of the hit man.

But what about when that threat was over? And was it over? She'd left Ark Crane in the jungle bleeding out. Likely he was dead by now. At least, she hoped he was dead by now.

But then there was the threat of Ridgewood. There were things she and Dane needed to talk about. Like was the man able to track them through time? And if so, how? And what was the larger machine he'd stepped inside and then disappeared? How much time had passed in their real world? Did it move linearly or not?

Even if she asked Dane, he wouldn't have answers either. They were stuck here together, after all. She had to stop dwelling on kissing him, or not kissing him, and pretend everything was situation normal between them. Honestly, she couldn't see herself with a man like Dane if they were in their real world. Their paths would never have crossed if it hadn't been for her father.

She huffed out a breath and flopped onto her stomach, curling around the satin pillow and pretending everything was normal. It was the last thing she thought before drifting off to sleep.

~ ☒ ~

Dane waited until she was deep asleep before dragging one of the chairs out to the terrace and settling down for the night. He stretched out his long legs, crossed them at the ankles and waited for sleep to come.

But it didn't. He was still wide awake when the eastern horizon lightened with the first hint of sunrise. At least in this world, in this time, the sun still rose in the east and set in the west.

As the sky changed from a deep indigo, to pale pink to blue, he got to his feet and moved to the terrace railing. He could clearly see the gardens in the first glint of morning light. They were as breathtaking as he imagined. Color popped everywhere. It was a virtual feast for the eyes as he took it all in. Flowers, shrubbery, a hedge maze, trees. Even the pathways seemed to have color. When the sun hit the pavestones, they sparkled with a pale pink hue.

For reasons he could not explain, all he wanted to do then was take Skye there and walk with her among the vibrant flora.

His tuned hearing picked up movement in the bedroom. He could hear the rustle of material, then her bare feet padding along the tile floor. He sensed her presence behind him, pausing in the doorway.

"Have you been out here all night?"

"Couldn't sleep," he said without turning.

She moved onto the terrace and joined him. He scented her, then, a faint aroma of something heady and sweet with which she'd washed her hair. Lilac.

"God, that's beautiful." Her voice was soft as she looked down at the gardens below. "I've never seen anything like it."

"The only thing I've seen that's come close are gardens in France."

He kept his gaze on the scenery before him. He didn't trust himself if he looked at her and see her disheveled, just-woke-up appearance. He didn't know want to know what she looked like first thing in the morning because then he would want to see her that way in the bed. Next to him. Naked.

"You've been to France?"

"Several times."

What he didn't tell her was that those times were when he worked a case. He never really traveled for pleasure. He never had time. He devoted years to the Army, then more years to the Secret Service. He spent his life serving others, his government, his country. He thought going into security for a private firm would give him the chance to put down roots. Perhaps that wasn't in the cards for him.

He hadn't thought of that since they started this whole mess. He thought he was getting into a slower pace of life as a consultant, that he would be able to stay in one place for a while, that he wouldn't have to be globetrotting or gallivanting all over the world. How wrong he was.

She leaned her forearms on the concrete railing and sighed, sounding wistful. "I've never been anywhere."

He looked at her then and it confirmed all his suspicions of her sexy morning look. God, but he hated the reaction he had to her. He needed to keep his head in check and his hands to himself. "That's not true."

She turned to look at him, her face upturned to him slightly. Her indigo eyes were inquisitive. "It's not?"

"You've been to fourteenth century Scotland and futuristic Russia." Places, he thought, they should never have been. Places that had, quite possibly, altered time.

A tiny smile lifted the corners of her full lips. "Yes, I suppose I have. Do those count?"

"They should."

She straightened, stretching her arms over her head and pulling her body taut. It gave him a lovely view of her shapely body. He looked away, taking interest again in the gardens below.

"Even though I didn't get a stamp in my passport, I guess it does." She yawned. "I've always wanted to travel. I got a passport when I was eighteen. Never used it."

She sounded saddened by that.

Dane thought of his own passport. It had plenty of stamps. He'd been all over the world. Through every third world shit hole, every major city, every jungle. Traveling for him had been a normal occurrence. Until the agency.

Idly, he wondered what was happening at the agency. Would they be looking for him? Wondering what happened to him? His ex-military boss would likely start at Goldenrod and follow his trail. Dane knew, though, at some point that trail would run cold unless he was able to connect with Thomas Hardy.

"Maybe someday you can use it." When he spoke, his voice was raspy, hoarse.

"Fat chance of that." She huffed out a breath. "We're stuck here, Dane. The broken time bender is never going to get us home."

"That's no way to think." He pulled the device from his pocket and held it out to her. She glared down at it as though it offended her. "We'll keep trying until we get home."

She lifted her gaze to his. "What if we never get home?"

He closed his hand around the device, trying to decide how to answer. It was a real possibility they'd be stuck together in time for eternity. What did he have to go back to?

A job he tolerated? A life of looking out for others who couldn't look out for themselves?

And what did she have to go back to? She was the orphaned former college girl. He knew for a fact she'd dropped all her classes after the death of her parents. He also knew she had no intention of returning despite the fact she told her professors she would after her grieving period. If she'd never received the time bender, if her father never hired him, if Ark Crane had never tried to kill her, would they even know each other?

"I suppose that's a real possibility," he said at last.

She gave him a sour look. "That's not very comforting."

"I know, but it's all I got." He wanted to reach for her, take her hand in his. Instead, he slipped the time bender back into his pocket and pressed his sweaty palms against the cool concrete railing.

"At least we have each other," she said, then. "I'd hate to be doing this alone."

Something sharp and hot pieced through his heart at her sincerity. "So would I."

He wanted to tell her they'd stick together no matter what but he couldn't make that kind of promise to her with Ridgewood hunting them. He had an advantage over them. He could see where they were going and when. He could find them with his machine. Dane was good at keeping people safe in his element. Here, he was far out of his element.

A knock on the door sounded, interrupting any more conversation. He was glad. He didn't want to talk about it anymore. Skye headed inside and opened the door. The princess stood on the other side. They spoke to each other, but he couldn't hear what they said. Their voices were nothing more than a low murmur. Skye closed the door and returned.

"The princess says Tia is awake. She's doing well."

"That's good." He was glad to see the relief in her face. For whatever reason, Skye had developed an attachment to the girl. "I'm glad to hear that."

"They're feasting in her honor this afternoon in the courtyard. They want us to attend."

"All right."

She hesitated, her hands on the railing. He sensed pent-up tension in her, as though she wanted to say more but couldn't or wouldn't.

"Skye, I'll get cleaned up. Then maybe we can check out those gardens before we have to be at the courtyard."

He wasn't sure what made him invite her to take a stroll through the gardens. He only knew he wanted to erase her thoughts of being trapped in time and give her a little piece of happiness if only for a brief time.

She looked at him a long moment and then finally gave him a soft smile. "I'd like that."

And so would he. Probably more than he should.

~ ⧗ ~

Skye was a bundle of energy. If she didn't do something about it soon, her skin was going to crack and split and she'd fall into a thousand tiny pieces.

What was she thinking? She couldn't walk with Dane alone in the gardens. He was… well…Dane.

If she could avoid him, she would but at the moment she was too busy pacing the length of the room while he took his time cleaning up. She ran her hands through her hair, pulling tangles out down to the ends. She dressed quickly when he disappeared to clean up and put on fresh clothes.

A knock on the door halted her pacing. She answered it to see Tia standing on the other side. Skye smiled but before she could say anything, the girl flung herself at her and hugged her hard.

"The princess told me what you did for me." Tia pulled back, held her at arm's length and searched her face.

"Which is?"

"You told her I wanted to go home." She gave her a tentative smile, as if she were unsure the statement was true.

"I did. I promised you, Tia."

Tia reached into her pocket and brought out a small heavy pouch. Coins clinked together. She pulled open the drawstring and showed her the contents. "She gave me this to buy clothes, food and passage. I told her I did not wish to feast."

Skye's mouth went dry. "You did? How did that go?"

"She and the king understood. They wish to send me to the docks." Tia closed the pouch and put it back in her pocket. She reached for Skye's hand and squeezed it. Her face beamed, her dark eyes alight with excitement and joy.

Skye couldn't help but smile at the girl's exuberance. "I'm happy for you, Tia."

"I could not have done this without you, *ta'rin*. For that, you have my eternal thanks." She bowed low.

"Tia, you don't have to call me *ta'rin* or bow to me. I'm just a girl like you." Well, not exactly like her. Tia had a power she didn't understand and would never have believed if she hadn't seen it with her own eyes.

"To me, you will always be *ta'rin da bara*." She granted her a small smile, then said, "There are horses waiting. I asked the princess if you and the man could see me to the docks."

Surprise flickered through her. "You mean now?"

The girl nodded.

Her heart sank a little. Despite her resistance not to walk alone with Dane in a romantic garden, she couldn't help but feel a little disappointed at the thought it wasn't going to happen now. Or was she relieved? Those two emotions warred within her. Skye pasted on a bright smile.

"Of course, we'll go with you."

"Where are we going?" Dane said from behind her. She didn't even know he'd entered the room.

Tia's gaze flickered to him and she gave him a low bow in greeting.

"We're going to take Tia to the docks." Skye kept her gaze focused on the girl as she spoke.

There was a pause, then he said, "What about the feast?"

"Canceled," Skye said.

She looked at him over her shoulder and her breath caught. He stood near the terrace doors, his black hair damp and freshly combed. He hadn't shaved in a few days, so he had the stubble on his face and jaw. Why had she not noticed that before? He wore a fresh tunic in burnt orange and pale brown pants. It took some effort to steady her voice when she spoke again.

"We're escorting Tia to her ship," Skye added.

"I see. Then we best be on our way." He walked toward them and motioned to the door.

Tia gave another curt nod before leaving the room. Skye met his sharp green gaze.

"I guess that garden walk will have to wait." She was unable to stop the words from flowing out of her moth.

"I guess so. Let's go."

He placed his warm hand on the middle of her back and gave her a gentle nudge out the door. With reluctance, Skye followed Tia down the hall wondering what Dane was thinking. Was he annoyed they weren't going to get that stroll through the garden? If he was, he didn't show it.

Tia led them out of the Citadel and down the long stone steps to the foot of the building where the king, queen, and princess waited next to three horses. Skye half expected to see Ridgewood with them, but he wasn't there and she was glad. They halted, Tia in front of her and Dane at her side.

The princess smiled and greeted Tia in their native tongue. She motioned to the horses then to Skye and Dane. Tia turned to her.

"The princess wishes me well and asks if you will return after seeing me safely to the ship," Tia said.

"Of course," Skye said.

Next to her, Dane stiffened. She suspected he was ready for them to move on and, truthfully, she was, too. They'd done all they could here in this strange world. It was time to go. Tia spoke again to the princess. They bowed to each other. Then the girl hoisted herself into the saddle of the nearest horse.

Skye glanced at Dane who gave her the go-ahead nod. As both settled in their saddles, Tia gave one last look at the Citadel and the royal family before turning her horse for the docks. She didn't look back again.

As they followed, Skye never looked back again either.

Chapter 15
Farewells

Ark Crane knew he was going to die. It was only a matter of time.

After Dane stabbed him and left him, he patched himself up as best as he could. He even managed to sew the wound with crude stitches. Stitches that had come out when he captured the girl. He could feel the blood seeping through the cloth he'd wrapped around his middle, soaking his shirt.

He laid on the floor of the jungle, staring up at the canopy of leaves overhead. The humidity pressed around him, nearly suffocating him. The twitter of birdsong surrounded him, the small winged creatures unaware of his dire situation. Weak and tired, he knew he would never get up from that place. He would die alone in a world he didn't belong.

"Get up, you filthy animal."

Ark's eyes shuttered closed. The last person he wanted to see was Charles Ridgewood. And yet he had returned for him despite his failure.

The sound of bracken underfoot signaled the arrival of the man next to him.

"Get up, I said."

"Can't," Ark said, his voice weak. "I'm busy dying."

Movement and the crunch of leaves. "He got you good, then." The nearness of his voice signaled he had kneeled next to him. Ridgewood pushed his arm out of the way and lifted the edge of his shirt. The man sucked in a sharp breath. "Looks bad."

"Told you. Dying."

Ridgewood inhaled a deep breath, as if deciding what he would do next. Ark cracked an eye and squinted at him, the afternoon sun shining behind his head like a halo. He almost laughed. Ridgewood was no savoir. He turned the small device over and over in his hand and he knew he had come back for him with the time bender instead of the machine that was to take them all back to their time.

"I can't let you die. I need you. We have unfinished work to do. They've time traveled again."

"I don't care," he said and meant it.

"Yes, you do. Because you want to live."

Not like this. He didn't want to live to serve Ridgewood and chase after those two through different worlds. He should have walked out of that interrogation room and let them kill him instead of accepting the job.

"The medical staff will take care of you as soon as we're back."

He twirled the dial on the tiny device and then placed his hand on his shoulder. Ridgewood pushed the button.

~ ⧗ ~

None of them spoke as they made their way through the village, down the mountain pathway and into the well-worn trail through the jungle. No one stopped them. No one bothered them. When they arrived at the docks, it was nothing like what Skye expected. She wasn't sure what she expected, though.

It was a thriving fishing village with ships at docks lined up for miles. Villagers bustled up and down the busy wharf doing whatever it was they needed to do. There was boisterous laughter between a captain and his crew as they disembarked. A girl dressed in a colorful full skirt and a form-fitting shirt carried a box of clams. Her shout in her native tongue was intended to lure customers.

The air smelled like salt and fish and ocean as a slight breeze lifted the stands of her unruly hair. She cut a glance at Dane, but he wasn't looking at her. He was looking at everyone and everything on the docks, taking it all in. She watched his hawk-like gaze touch on it all, making mental notes. His hands gripped the reins so tight, veins stood out along the backs of his hands and his forearms were rigid and his muscles were taut. She could see the stiff line of his shoulders and his ramrod straight back as he sat in the saddle.

He was on edge.

She glanced around at all the colorful, happy, people trying to see what he saw. But she saw nothing out of the ordinary.

Tia reined her horse to a stop and dismounted. She looked up at her, the sun bright on her face. "The ship I'll be leaving on is just there." She pointed to the one at the end. "I'm going to speak with the captain."

"Should we come with you?" Skye asked.

"No." She shook he head. "I'll only be a moment."

Taking her horse by the reins, she led it over to the captain, the same one that had the boisterous laughter as they rode onto the wharf. Dane dismounted, patting his horse's neck. Skye remained in the saddle. It didn't escape her notice he was still surveying the area.

"I think we should leave, too," he said.

"You mean, use the machine?"

"Yes," he said.

Skye watched Tia talk to the captain. He eyed her horse and asked a question. She nodded. He reached for the reins, then turned to one of his men and spoke. The man took the horse and led it onto the ship. She motioned back toward her and Dane and he gave a nod. As Tia hurried back to them, she got down off her horse.

"I have secured passage for me and my horse on the ship *The Valiant*." Her face was alight with joy as she hugged Skye. "I will miss you."

"I'll miss you, too, but I know you'll be glad to get home."

She pulled away, gave her a nod. "Thank you again." Then she glanced over at Dane. "And thank you, too."

It was awkward between them, Skye noticed. He hadn't spent as much time with the girl as Skye had, so he merely gave her a nod and a smile.

"You're welcome."

"May you both find good fortune." Holding Skye's hands, she squeezed them tight before releasing her.

"And may you as well," Skye said.

One more farewell and the girl headed for the ship. Skye watched her walk up the gangway and board and then she was gone. She didn't know why, but it hurt to see her go. Dane moved to stand next to her.

"Hopefully she'll be all right on that ship full of men," he said.

"I hope so, too." Her stomach clenched as she realized what could happen to the lovely young woman. It hadn't really occurred to her that Tia put herself in a dangerous situation by boarding a ship full of roughened men who looked like nothing more than pirates. "Maybe I should have talked her out of it. Told her she should stay at the Citadel and be their *ta'rin da bara*."

"I don't think she would have listened, Skye," he said. "She had it in her mind she was going home and that's all she wanted to do."

Home. She turned to face him. "Can *we* go home now?"

He slipped his hand in his pocket and brought out the small device with the faded digital screen. The numbers were almost impossible to read now. He flicked it on with the tip of his thumb.

"We can try. That's all we can do."

They both stared down at the device.

"And if we end up somewhere else?" she asked.

He placed his other hand under her chin and tipped her head back. She looked into those depthless green eyes of his. "We stick together. No matter what."

"No matter what." She gave a nod.

He wrapped his arm around her, pulled her to him, and suddenly the sights and sounds of the busy wharf disappeared. She wrapped an arm around his waist, standing so close to him she could smell the scent of the soap he'd used that morning in the bathing chamber. Citrus.

She focused on the little time bender in his hand. With her free hand, she clasped his hand holding the device, her thumb on top of his hovering over the button. Then she lifted her face to his and kissed his roughened cheek.

"For luck," she whispered.

Together, they pushed the button.

Epilogue

Thomas turned down the dirt road that led to the abandoned farmhouse. Next to him, Harold was silent as they bumped along. He pulled the pickup into the rundown barn and then hopped out and walked to the open doorway. He stood there a moment, surveying the surroundings to make sure he wasn't followed. He saw nothing and no one. Only the sounds of birds twittering and a slight breeze. He pulled the barn door closed and turned back to the pickup.

Harold retrieved the bags of groceries, grabbing two in each hand. Thomas picked up the rest of them and headed to one side of the barn, the kid on his heels. He kicked open a hatch in the floor and motioned for Harold to go down.

The kid peered down the hole for a long moment before maneuvering his way down the shaky ladder, somehow managing to hold onto the full plastic bags as he made his way down. Thomas followed. It wasn't easy, for sure. Harold waited at the bottom of the ladder and then followed him through his underground living quarters to the small kitchen.

Thomas converted the root cellar into a livable space. He managed to get the electricity working and added an apartment-size refrigerator to the little kitchenette. It was far from perfect, but better than nothing. He added a counter with a hot plate and a few dishes, a large sink that looked more like a converted tub. He had to haul water from the well outside to wash dishes and forget about bathing. The last time he managed a shower was when he visited a truck stop two days ago.

"You live here?" Harold's disdain was apparent as he looked around the crude surroundings.

"You can call it living but it's more like existing," Thomas replied.

He placed the bags on the rickety card table he used as a dining table. Four chairs that had seen better days surrounded it. He unloaded the food and put away the cold items first. Harold glanced around the small area, his gaze halting on first the workstation he'd set up for himself and then the narrow bed shoved against a corner. The kid approached the workstation.

"Don't touch anything," Thomas warned.

He stuck his hands in his pockets. "I wasn't." But his gaze was intent on the two widescreen monitors. "Where did you get all this stuff?"

"I'm borrowing it."

In truth, he'd stolen the best pieces from the old tech building before he hightailed it out of the city. He hadn't had much time to figure out how to get Skye and Dane home—or even if he could—because he was busy making backup plans in case he had to leave at a moment's notice. When he finished putting away the food, he turned to Harold.

"You said you could help me find them."

Harold nodded. "I did, and I can." He motioned to the keyboard. "May I?"

Thomas hesitated. Finally, he nodded.

Harold sat at the desk and clicked on the computer. The login screen came up. He cut a glance at Thomas who was already at his side. He nudged him out of the way and typed in the password. The screen opened with the program showing the location of the time bender he'd left running. Harold leaned toward the monitor and squinted, as if that would make it come into focus better.

"This doesn't make sense," the kid said.

"Yeah, it didn't to me either."

"This data indicates time has somehow…bent…around them." Harold looked up at Thomas, question in his youthful eyes. "I don't get it."

"I didn't either until I remembered one of the testing phases. Will discovered a way not only to time travel, but also hit parallel universes. I think that's what happened with their latest time jump."

His face blanched as he looked back at the screen. "That's impossible."

"No, it's not, because Skye and Dane did it. Wherever they are, they didn't time travel linearly."

"Then…where are they?"

"I thought you said you read all the research?" Thomas said, his tone laced with accusation.

"I did but there was nothing in the notes about this." He pointed to the screen and the green arc indicating bent time.

He was right, there wasn't. William Ransom never wrote it down when he discovered it as a real possibility. It was something only a few of them knew. One of them Conner Dade.

"You said you saw the plans for the second prototype?" he asked.

The kid nodded. "Yeah, that and…something else."

He didn't like the sound of that. "What something else?"

"Janus Force figured out how to build a bigger machine to carry more than one person through time."

Thomas stared at him in disbelief as his stomach cramped. They'd figured out how to build a large machine using William Ransom's notes? Unreal. And dangerous.

"That's the other thing I wanted to tell you, but I didn't want to say it out loud in public."

He ran a hand through his hair and paced to the small fridge. He pulled out a beer, popped the top and downed a healthy swig. This was information he wasn't prepared for or expecting.

"Can I have one of those?"

Thomas cut him a glance. "How old are you, kid?"

"Old enough."

He rose from the desk and joined him at the fridge. Thomas reached in and handed him one. He opened it, took a sip, made a face.

"You don't even like beer, do you?"

"No, but I think the alcohol will be necessary if we're going to figure out how to get them home."

"I'm open to suggestions," Thomas said.

"I have a few ideas." The kid put down the can and walked back to the computer. He sat and tapped out commands on the keyboard then stopped. He stared at the screen for a long moment before his head snapped over to Thomas. "You can track the second one, too?"

He nodded. He hadn't looked at the tracking for the second device since Skye and Dane time jumped. He figured whoever used it was following the two of them through time, so he didn't think it was pertinent at the time. Buying food was more important.

Harold sat back in the chair and stared at the screen. "That changes things a bit. Not in a bad way either."

Thomas was about to ask him another question when they heard the muffled sound of a car door slam. Harold stiffened, his eyes flying to the open hatch. Thomas hurried to the ladder, climbed up and halted at the top enough to poke his head out. He slammed the hatch closed and jumped to the floor.

"Do not make a sound," Thomas whispered.

He crept to the workstation and clicked off both monitors, plunging the cellar in shadowed darkness. Above them, they could hear footsteps on the wooden barn floor. Slow. Methodical. The truck door opened. A long silence and Thomas knew whoever it was rifled through the cab of the pickup. They would find nothing. He kept no identifying information inside it. The door slammed. More footsteps halting right over their heads.

"Mr. Hardy? I know you're here. My name is Nick Slaughter. I work with Dane Fortune. I need your help finding him."

Thomas met Harold's gaze, but he couldn't see the kid's expression. Should he take a chance? Should he open the hatch and let the guy know he was there? He didn't know anything about Dane Fortune, only that he was hired to protect William Ransom. If Nick was coming to look for them then surely, they were business partners. And if he was looking for Dane, then maybe he could help them somehow. At the very least, maybe this person could move him out of this shit hole and get him a decent setup and protection from whoever this Janus Force was. Because it was only a matter of time before they, too, found him.

"I followed his trail and I know he and the girl talked to you. I need to know where they are."

Decision made, Thomas climbed the ladder and shoved open the hatch. The man stood above him, surprise flickering over his features as he saw Thomas ascend the remaining rungs and step out into the barn.

Nick Slaughter was tall with short-cropped sandy hair, a weathered face that showed he'd been to hell and back and piercing blue hawk-like eyes that missed nothing. He wore a white button-down shirt with the collar open and sleeves rolled to his elbows, black pants and black combat boots. Stubble lined his square jaw and cheeks. If G.I. Joe was a real person, he would be it.

"How do I know you're telling the truth?" Thomas asked.

He reached into his pocket and brought out a business card, handed it over. Thomas looked down at the gold foil lettering of the company Peregrine Protection Agency and an embossed falcon logo. Below Nick's name was the title Owner followed by two phone numbers and an email address.

"This doesn't mean you're legit. Anyone can create a business card."

He gave him a faint smile. "You're cautious. I get it and I appreciate that, but I need your help. I have a case file with all the details on the William Ransom job. Dane was hired to protect him. He told me he intended to protect the daughter despite the fact he wasn't getting paid for it. That was the day they disappeared. You're the last person to see them both alive. You, and the hit man, Conner Dade, hired."

Thomas knew what he said was true. That or he was good at ferreting out information. Either way, he would proceed with caution.

"I haven't heard from him in days. His apartment looks like he hasn't been back there since. Same with the girl's house."

Thomas still didn't answer as he peered at the man, trying to decide if he could trust him. "I don't know where they are." It was, at least the truth. But a half truth.

He huffed out a breath. "I know you don't trust me but you're the last link I have to my agent and I need answers."

"And you think I have them?"

"I hoped you would."

He considered the man. What did he have to lose? A lot. He could be making a huge mistake by even talking to him. For all he knew, Janus Force sent him. But then, if that were true, why not just kill him and get it over with?

On the flipside, he had a lot to gain by helping him and his agency. He would have resources and connections Thomas only dreamed about. Tentative trust flickered through him.

"Then, Mr. Slaughter, perhaps we can help each other."

# # #

Skye and Dane's adventure will continue in
Volume 4: Lord of the Underworld

Sneak Peak of Lord of the Underworld, Vol 4!

Traveling through time sucked. It was quite possibly the worst thing Skye had ever done. If they ever got home, she made a promise to herself she would never leave again.

"Can *we* go home now?"

Dane slipped his hand out of his pocket and brought out the small device that had become the bane of their existence. She was beginning to hate the little thing. He flicked it on with the tip of his thumb.

"We can try. That's all we can do."

They both peered down at the thing in his hand. "And if we end up somewhere else?" she asked.

He placed his warm fingers under her chin and tipped her head back. She looked up into his depthless green eyes. He cocked a grin at her.

"We stick together no matter what."

She nodded. "No matter what."

He wrapped an arm around her and pulled her close. She clasped his hand holding the device, her thumb hovering over the top of his. She kissed Dane's scruffy face. The prickly sensation of his cheek made her lips throb. "For luck."

He gave her a quick smile and together they pushed the button, leaving the Citadel behind. She hoped they would end up closer to home. But coming awake after the violence of falling through time made her groan.

Heat pounded through her as she peeled her eyes open and tried to focus on her surroundings. Above her, a brilliant blue cloudless sky. Somewhere nearby she could hear the soft lapping of water. Not like an ocean. More like that of a lake. She flung out her arm to feel the ground next to her. Her hand plopped into cool water. She rolled over and peered through cattails.

Where had they ended up this time?

She sat up, glancing around looking for Dane but he was nowhere in sight. They had pushed the button together but that didn't mean they would end up together. They'd been separated before. It was never a good thing. Dane was her protector and the only one she really trusted. Hell, he was the only one along for the ride with her so she *had* to trust him.

Not that she had any reason not to trust him. In wintertime, he'd rescued her from the crazy tribesman who wanted to marry her and then sacrifice her. In the Citadel, he'd managed to keep her safe from Charles Ridgewood and whatever he was up to.

She thought of Ridgewood now, of the strange machine he'd disappeared in, and wondered if he would be back. He seemed desperate to take her back with him. She had no idea what he wanted from her or why.

"Dane?"

She kept her voice low in case there were natives who wanted to do her harm. After everything they had been through, she'd learned to always stay on her guard. In the distance, she could hear a rhythmic thumping that sounded like a drum. She got to her knees and peered over the tops of the cattails.

Calm, blue water stretched between her and the other side of the river. On the opposite shore, she could see a processional. In the lead, a man banging a drum in a *thump, thump, thump*. Behind him, two men dressed in long scarlet colored robes, sandals, and a thick golden choker around their neck. Each wore a tall square-shaped headdress and carried a long pole with a red and gold banner flapping in the wind. Painted in the center of each banner was the silhouette of what reminded her of an Anubis.

Behind the two men, three women. All dressed in opaque flowing gowns in various earth-tone colors of red, orange, gold. The woman in the center wore black and had her head bowed in grief, her dark hair covered in jewels dripping down her back. Behind her, the four men carried what looked like a crude stretcher with a body swathed in gauze. Behind them, more men armed with swords and spears.

It was a funeral procession and, by the looks of it, the deceased had been someone important. She kneeled there on the edge of the water, watching as they made their way along the bank of the river. She leaned forward through the cattails to see they were headed toward a large stone temple carved into the side of the mountain. No doubt a tomb.

Fascinating.

Had they somehow landed in Ancient Egypt? If their time traveling history was any indication, it could be another alternate universe like the Citadel. Remembering the little device, she glanced around for the time bender. She ran her hand through the damp grass looking for it but came up empty handed.

Hot fear trickled over her. While Dane had held the device, they had both pushed the button. Hopefully, he still had the thing so they could get out of here when it reset itself.

"Dane?" she called again, this time a little louder.

A nearby groan gave her hope.

"I'm here," she said.

She could hear the splashing of water and then Dane's head popped up through the cattails. He was soaked from head to toe. Relief washed through her, though. At least he was still there with her.

"Are you all right?" She made her way over to him.

He nodded, patting himself down. "I think so. No broken bones or injuries."

"Do you still have the time bender?"

He met her gaze, his green eyes bright with concern. He got back down on his hands and knees and searched the area.

With her heart in her throat, she hurried over to him, dropped to her knees next to him, and helped him search.

"I had it," he said, "when we jumped."

"I know." Her voice warbled with the fear the damn thing was lost and they'd be stuck there. Wherever there was.

He stuck his hand under the surface, disturbing the silt and turning the clear water cloudy. He froze and lifted his gaze to her. She didn't like that look at all. When he lifted his hand, it dripped mud and water. In his palm, the soiled time bender.

"Well, shit." It was the only thing she could think to say as she stared at the muddy little device.

He brushed away the mud. "The screen still works, if that's any consolation."

"Not really." Hot tears burned the backs of her eyes as she stared at the device. There was no way to know if the thing was waterproof or mud proof. "Now what?"

"I guess we wait the three days and see if it resets itself."

"And if it doesn't?" She hated asking the question, but she had to.

He said nothing as he slowly shook his head. He didn't want to voice the answer as much as she didn't want to hear it. Skye sank to the ground, not caring if she was sitting in the middle of a marshy puddle surround by cattails. A dragonfly fluttered across her vision, but she couldn't focus on it through the sudden tears that watered her eyes.

"We're never getting home, are we?" She sounded pathetic. She knew it. But she couldn't help it.

"Never is a strong word, I'd say." He used his wet tunic to further clean the device. He scraped away the mud with the edge of his tunic. "You're giving up too easily."

Don't miss any of Skye and Dane's Adventures!

***Highland Fling*, Volume 1**

A girl, a hit man and a time machine may be more than Dane Fortune can handle.

"…characters with real chemistry and a rip-roaring adventure." —5 stars, Amazon Reviewer

"…a fun twist to time travel…" —4 stars, Amazon Reviewer

"Dane Fortune is a delicious blend of everything you want in a hero." —4 stars, BookBub Reviewer

"I liked the set up for this book. It's pretty exciting and I didn't want to put it down." —5 stars, Amazon Reviewer

***Dead of Winter*, Volume 2**

At the mercy of a faulty time machine, will Skye and Dane be able to make it home alive?

"…heart-stopping…full of anxiety-inducing moments and nail-biting suspense." —5 stars, BookBub Reviewer

"…a fun adventure that will leave [you] wanting more Ransom and Fortune." —4 stars, Amazon Reviewer

"…you'll want book 1 first so you can join in the wild ride from the beginning." —5 stars, BookBub Reviewer

"Adding the element of time travel to a book already rife with fantastical events—the story's endless possibilities are spellbinding." —Fort Worth Magazine

The Citadel, Volume 3

Still lost in time, Skye and Dane face their most dangerous enemy yet.

"What an amazing and addicting series!" —5 stars, Amazon Reviewer

"... plenty of action and a great storyline kept me reading until I finished it!" —5 stars, Amazon Reviewer

"Can't wait for the next one!" —5 stars, Amazon Reviewer

Lord of the Underworld, Volume 4

This title has never been published before and is a brand new adventure!

"This was a fast paced read..." —4 stars, Amazon Reviewer

"...a fast paced time travel adventure that is such a fun and easy read." —5 stars, Amazon Reviewer

"...a well written story that kept me turning pages, I want to read the next book." —4 stars, BookBub Reviewer

Praise for the Dragon Protectors

Desiring the Dragon Lord, Book 1

"Michelle Miles kicks off her new Dragon Protectors series with a bang…" —4 stars, Amazon Reviewer

"I read this book in just a couple of days. I couldn't put it down!" —5 stars, Amazon Reviewer

"…a wonderful book full of strong minded characters." —5 stars, Amazon Reviewer

Seducing the Dragon Knight, Book 2

"From the start this book has danger and a bit of mystery." —4 stars, Amazon Reviewer

"I love this author and this genre. A must read." —5 stars, Booksprout Reviewer

"I was half in love with Rafe when we met him in Desiring the Dragon Lord, but oh get me a fan and a cool drink, because his hot factor increased 100-fold in the second installment." —4 stars, Amazon Reviewer

Tempting Her Dragon Bodyguard, Book 3

"I loved reading this book and hope there are more to come." —5 stars, Amazon Reviewer

"Book three in the Dragon Protectors series a well written story that kept me turning pages. I had to know what was going to happen." —5 stars, Amazon Reviewer

"…a captivating storyline…" —4 stars, Amazon Reviewer

Praise for Age of Wizards

In the Tower of the Wizard King, **Book 1**

"The book has a very strong and intriguing plotline as well as unforgettable characters. I liked the parallel narration of the present and the past as it made the story both more complicated and more involving…" —5 stars, Amazon Reviewer

"The mix of past and present stories brings the reader full circle and will keep you engrossed in the story. Beware though, you may not want to put the book down! …two thumbs up…!" —5 stars, Goodreads Reviewer

"Michelle Miles brilliantly weaves twists and turns, love stories both past and present, secrets, betrayal and revenge, with multi-dimensional characters, two different timelines and two different worlds." —5 stars, Amazon Reviewer

"I thoroughly enjoyed every aspect of this book, and highly recommend it. Filled with fantasy and three dimensional characters I couldn't put it down." —5 stars, Amazon Reviewer

On the Hunt for the Wizard King, **Book 1**

"We really got to watch all of the characters grow and change throughout the book. No one was what you expected. Miles did a great job of keeping you guess and wondering what was around the next corner." —5 stars, Amazon Reviewer

"Wow! This story is so full of magic with action and adventure I could not put it down. The land of fae is an exciting magical world where anything can happen, and I definitely was not expecting some of the twist and turns that transpired." —5 stars, Amazon Reviewer

Also by Michelle Miles

Dream Walker
Call of the Dark

Age of Wizards
In the Tower of the Wizard King
On the Hunt for the Wizard King

A Ransom & Fortune Adventure
Highland Fling, Vol 1
Dead of Winter, Vol 2
The Citadel, Vol 3
Lord of the Underworld, Vol 4

Dragon Protectors
Desiring the Dragon Lord
Seducing the Dragon Knight
Tempting Her Dragon Bodyguard

Realm of Honor
One Knight Only
Only for a Knight
A Knight to Remember
A Knight Like No Other
Shadows of the Knight

Guardians of Atlantis
Tempting Eden
Seducing Eve
Ravishing Helene
Guardians of Atlantis Box Set

Coffee House Chronicles
Talk Dirty to Me
Nice Girls Do
Have Yourself a Merry Little Latte
Take Me I'm Yours
Sex, Lust & Martinis

Forever Yours
A Little Taste of Heaven

Shorts and Anthologies
A Dance Among the Faeries, Short Story
Eorwulf, Short Story
The Soul of Sharah, Short Story
Sinfully Sweet, Short Story
Flights of Fantasy: A Collection of Short Stories

Watch for more at www.MichelleMiles.net

About the Author

Michelle Miles believes in fairy tales, true love and magic. She is the award-winning author of the epic fantasy, IN THE TOWER OF THE WIZARD KING, as well as the fantasy romance series, REALM OF HONOR, featuring knights and their ladies fair, and the paranormal dragon-shifter romance series, DRAGON PROTECTORS.

In her spare time, she enjoys listening to music, reading, cross-stitching and watching movies. Even though she's a native Texan, she loves castles, dragons, fairies and elves and is an avid Game of Thrones fan. She can be found online at Facebook, Twitter, Instagram, Pinterest, and Goodreads.